Doctor's Delight

A River's End Ranch Story
Kirsten Osbourne

Sign up for instant notification of all of Kirsten's New Releases Text 'BOB' to 42828

And

For a complete list of Kirsten's works head to her website wwww.kirstenandmorganna.com

Chapter One

Steven Pickman stood looking out over the valley where River's End Ranch was located. From his vantage point on the side of one of the mountains overlooking the ranch, it looked picturesque, covered in snow as it was. He'd been staying on the ranch for three days so far, and he was pretty sure this was where they'd film the new show. He wasn't quite sure what they'd call the series yet, but he knew it was going to be a good one.

When someone had sent him the book *Mail Order Miracle*, based on the people who had first settled the ranch, he'd known they had to base a series on it, and he'd immediately signed on as one of the shows executive producers. So he was there checking out possible filming locations while he was on a three-week hiatus from filming Lazy Love, a show he'd been directing for five years.

He took a step closer to the edge, trying to get a better view, and his foot slipped. He tumbled head over heels down, rolling as he went. When he landed, he groaned at the pain he was feeling. He put his hand into his pocket and pulled out his phone, calling 911. After describing his location to the best of his ability, he prayed. He'd left his coat laying over the snowmobile. He didn't know if he was more likely to freeze to death or starve to death before he was found, but he knew he couldn't climb that mountain to get to his coat.

He'd heard rumors that Bigfoot lived in these mountains, and he was hoping he found better help than a giant furry ape-man, but he'd take what he could get at that moment.

He wasn't sure how long he laid there in the snow, but it seemed like both ten minutes and an hour. A young woman on a snowmobile with a toboggan pulled behind, stopped beside him. Two men followed on one snowmobile and stopped to help.

The woman knelt beside him. "I'm Dani, one of the Westons. I'm with Search and Rescue. The sheriff, who's also my brother-in-law, called me to try and find you."

He blinked at her, the sun shining right behind her, and it was hard to see her. "Thank you!"

"How badly are you hurt?" she asked, frowning down at him. "We don't want to move you until we're sure you're all right."

"I don't think anything's broken. I'm just bruised and really cold. Good thing is, there shouldn't be any swelling since I've been lying in the snow for so long."

Dani grinned. "Sounds like you're ready for us to get you down this mountain then, huh? I'm wondering if we take you straight to the hospital in Riston, or if we should just take you to the nurse at our first aid. Any thoughts on that?"

"Let's start with the nurse, and see where she thinks I should go."

"Perfect." Dani looked over her shoulder. "My friends here are going to get you on the toboggan, and I'm going to carefully drive down the mountain with you. We'll take you to Bridget, our nurse. Her sister calls her Bridget the Midget."

Steven smiled. "Sounds like she's going to be an interesting character. Or maybe just her sister is."

"Her sister's a romance writer who lives close to the ranch, too. She actually wrote a romance about my ancestors, the first Westons who settled this ranch. She's a lot of fun." Dani kept talking as they loaded him onto the toboggan. He wasn't sure if she was talking to distract him, or if she was just one that liked to hear the sound of her own voice. "It's actually the only romance I've ever read, but I enjoyed it. Maybe because it was about my ancestors."

He started to tell her it was a good book, but at the moment, he wasn't sure if this was the place he wanted to shoot. He needed to keep quiet about his purpose there for just a little bit longer.

When he was strapped in, Dani straddled her machine. "The snowmobile I rented is up there!" he called, wanting to make sure they could find it.

"My friends will get it down. Don't worry about that!" The motor started and he was riding along. It was a strange way to travel, lying on his back and staring up at the sky. He couldn't decide if he liked it or if it creeped him out. So he closed his eyes and slept, knowing he'd need his strength later.

STEVEN WOKE UP TO A tiny little woman directing two new men to put him onto a table. "I have a feeling we're going to be sending him to the hospital, but I want to look first. I can't do x-rays here."

"Nothing's broken," Steven told them.

"Are you sure?" Bridget asked, surprised. "I know you took quite a fall, and they said you couldn't get up."

"I couldn't at first, with the wind knocked out of me. I couldn't later because I was too cold. Give me a few minutes to warm up, and I can walk." He hated hospitals, and he'd do anything to avoid them. *Anything.*

"Okay, I'll give you a few." She walked away from him for a moment, and came back with a couple of heat pads. "I'm going to put these on you to help you warm up quicker. I'm Bridget, by the way. I'm the nurse here on the ranch, and I run the first aid station located in the old town apothecary shop.

He looked around him, and everything looked very modern to him. "I don't think the inside of your building matches the outside."

Bridget laughed. "Not exactly. Do you want it to?"

"I don't really think so." He moved the heat pad all around him, doing his very best to warm up—at least a little. The heat was painful with as cold as he'd been, but it was a pain worth suffering through.

Finally, he rolled to his side and sat up slowly, Bridget watching him with wide eyes. "How bad is the pain?"

He shrugged. "Low back isn't happy, but that's the worst of it."

Bridget tilted her head to one side, watching him. "I'll give you a choice then. You can go into town to the ER and have one of the doctors there give you muscle relaxers and pain pills to make it through, or you can go see our resident chiropractor."

He'd never seen a chiropractor—and he'd always thought of them as quacks—but hospitals gave him the creeps. He was willing to do just about anything to not go to the hospital. "Chiropractor it is."

She grinned. "I'm not a fan of hospitals either. Let's go to my car, and I'll drive you over. It's not far, but I'm not sure if you're up to walking at the moment."

"Probably not." He slid off the table very carefully and walked with her to her car. "Getting in is going to be a trick."

"Take your time. She's got twenty minutes until she closes."

"A female chiropractor?"

Bridget started the car. "Yup. And she's the best I've ever seen, so you can get your bad attitude right out of your head."

Steven said nothing else as he carefully lowered his body enough to get into her car and swung his legs in. He wanted to cheer when he'd finished, because it had felt like a herculean effort. He hoped the chiropractor was as good as Bridget claimed.

DR. MICHELLE PETERS looked around her office as she was finishing up for the day. She ran a chiropractic practice out of a spa on River's End Ranch in Northern Idaho. While she loved her job, sometimes she wished she could help more people, because the ranch was a guest ranch, and there were different people in and out every week.

She put the few charts she'd worked with that day into a filing cabinet and walked toward the front door, planning to run out just five minutes early. Meeting a few friends for pizza and trivia that night sounded better than sitting alone in her office hoping someone would come to see her.

Michelle stopped with her hand on the doorknob, wondering if it was time for her to move on. While she loved the ranch and the crazy people it attracted, she wasn't doing the kind of work she'd gone to school for. She'd really thought she'd be helping people overcome injuries. Instead she had time between patients.

The door was pushed in, and Bridget came in with a man she'd never seen before. "Did you bring me a patient?"

Bridget nodded. "He fell quite a distance down the mountain. Says there's nothing broken, but his low back is painful. He was in the snow for about an hour before Dani found him."

Michelle nodded. "All right, but the first thing I'm going to do is x-rays. I want to make sure I'm not going to damage you worse by adjusting you."

"I'm going back to the first aid station. I have another couple of hours before Kevin comes to take me away from all of the hustle and bustle of broken people."

Bridget had always seemed a bit over-dramatic to Michelle, so she just nodded. "Thanks for bringing me this guy." Michelle looked at him. "What's your name anyway?"

"Steven Pickman. I'm a guest here on the ranch."

"I figured you were. I know everyone who lives here."

He nodded, his low back feeling as if it was on fire. "I'm sure you do. It's a pretty sparsely populated area." Which would be perfect for the show if they decided this was the right location.

"Follow me into an exam room. I'm going to have you do some bends and stretches to see what the extent of your injury seems to be, and then we'll do x-rays."

After the exam and x-rays, she nodded. "Well, I'm pretty sure I can help you. I'm going to do an adjustment on you. Have you ever seen a chiropractor?"

He shook his head. "Nope. Just assumed they were all quacks."

Michelle laughed. "I thought the same thing. While I adjust you, I'm going to tell you my chiropractic story, and you're going to listen, because you really don't have a choice." So as she moved her hand up and down his spine, searching for places he needed adjusted—and there were a lot because of his fall—she talked to him. "When I was in college, I was pre-med. I wanted to be a general practitioner, but I was a gymnast, and my scholarship was paying my way through college. I had an accident doing a back flip one day, and I hurt my back. I went to see a doctor, and he couldn't really help me. Then a friend told me to see a chiropractor, and I told her they were quacks."

"Ow!" Steven yelled as she jerked him in a way he hadn't expected.

"Sorry, not sorry," Michelle said. "Anyway, I finally agreed, and it took him three weeks to fix the pain that a regular doctor hadn't helped in six months. So I went to chiropractic school instead of medical school."

When she finished adjusting him, and had him bend once more. "That's a little better."

"Well, it will be a lot better soon, I hope. How long are you here?" she asked.

"Another week. Why?"

"Because I need to see you at least a couple of more times before you go back to where you came from. Where did you come from anyway?" Michelle was curious about him. Most people didn't travel to a place like River's End on their own.

"I live in California, but I direct a television show in Texas."

"Really? Anything I would have heard of?"

"Lazy Love." The show was constantly winning Emmy awards, so he knew she'd have at least heard of it.

"Oh, I watched one episode of that. Not a fan."

He blinked a few times. No one had ever told him that. "Really? But you only watched one show?" How could she know if she liked it if she hadn't given it a chance?

"Yeah, but I make up my mind pretty fast." She led him to the front desk. "I want to see you around ten tomorrow morning. I know you're going to be sore, but I need to adjust you again, and show you some exercises to do. We'll have you feeling better within a week."

He sighed. "All right." He really didn't want to have to come back to her. Her hands were strong, and she'd hurt him. But he didn't want to live with the pain or go to the hospital either. She seemed to be the lesser of the evils.

Michelle watched him for a moment. "I missed my plans to play trivia with my friends tonight, but we can slip in and help a bit if you want. Do you have plans?"

He shook his head. "I don't really know anyone here." He was on a business trip, but finding out more about the ranch and what the locals did could only help. "Yeah, I'll go."

"Sounds good. Let me just lock up, and we'll head over to the restaurant." She walked with long strides down the hall and realized she was leaving the injured man in her dust. "Oh, sorry. Forgot you were all gimpy. Do you want to drive over? It's a five-minute walk, but that might be a bit too much for you."

He shrugged. "I would probably do better in the car tonight."

"If you get too sore at trivia, you're welcome to leave. I understand that you're in pain today."

"All right." He did his best to keep pace beside her, but she was tall, and her legs seemed to go on forever.

She drove him to the restaurant, and then waited as he slowly got out of the car. "Were you on the mountain by yourself?"

He nodded. "I called 911 as soon as I fell."

"Smart man. You'd have been lying there a whole lot longer if you hadn't." She walked into the restaurant and looked around for her spa friends. Karen was there, and so was their new massage therapist, Tricia. "There're my friends. The ranch usually only does trivia on Thursday nights, but people have been asking for more evenings. They threw this one here to see if there'd be a good turn-out, and it looks like there is. Monday nights weren't expected to be good, though."

Steven quickly realized he was going to be the only guy at the table, but since he was there to observe people it really didn't matter. He looked around him, spotting Dani, the girl who had rescued him. She was with a girl who looked remarkably like her but with blonder hair, and two tall, strong-looking men. "Who's that with Dani?" he asked Michelle.

Michelle looked over at the table in question. "Oh, that's her twin sister Kelsi and both of their husbands. The one in the sheriff's uniform is Kelsi's husband, and the one dressed more casually is Travis, Dani's husband."

Well, that explained how much the two women looked alike. He would have guessed sisters, but not twins. Looking at them more closely, he could see they had the same face. "They're part of the Weston family?"

Michelle nodded. "Yeah. Wade is over there with his wife, Maddie," she said, pointing across the room. "And that's Will over there, with his wife Ellie. Wyatt isn't here, but they have a young baby. I think Kelsi's twins and Will's newborn must be with Mrs. Weston, as well as Maddie and Wade's girl." She looked around a little more. "I don't see Wes either. Must be off somewhere else tonight."

"Does the family usually participate in all of the activities?"

"Yeah, a lot of times. I mean not always, because they do have lives away from the ranch, but they all feel really strongly about this place." She frowned for a moment, thinking. "You know, I think the little ones must be with Debbie in the Kids' Korral. I think Mr. And Mrs. Weston are in the RV this month, seeing the world."

"Do they do that a lot?" Steven knew he was asking a lot of questions, but before he actually signed a deal with these people, he wanted to know as much as he could about them.

"Usually they go off every other month. Mrs. Weston wants to spend lots of time here with her grandbabies, so they were here from Thanksgiving through New Years', and they took off yesterday, I believe. They've turned the ranch over to the kids, who all share responsibility for it, so they aren't really needed for the day-to-day operations."

"I see. I didn't realize they were no longer at the helm." The research he'd done hadn't indicated a change of ownership, but he wasn't sure how old the research was.

"Yeah, they turned the ranch over as part of the Halloween party this past year. The kids have really been running it for a couple of years, but their parents kept interfering. They don't do that anymore." Michelle looked over at her friends, who were obviously struggling with a question. "What is it?"

Karen made a face. "I don't know those old movies. 'According to *Singing in the Rain*, what does Moses think his toeses are?' What are toeses?"

Michelle grinned, and she and Steven said at the same time, "Roses!"

They looked at each other and laughed. "*Singing in the Rain* fan?" she asked.

"Movie fan. Old, new, it doesn't matter. I just love movies and TV shows both."

"I guess you have to, with your occupation. I might have to try that show of yours again."

"You really should. If you like it, I'll make sure you get an autographed poster from the show."

"Oh, that would be fun. I've met May, who married the guy who plays Bob."

"Oh yeah, I know May. She's really good for Bob." Steven smiled, thinking about two of his favorite people.

"No, I mean the guy who *plays* Bob." Michelle frowned at him. She couldn't think of the actor's name, and she'd been sure he'd know.

"Yeah, Bob plays Bob. It's a joke all across the set. May is super nice. Bob can't quit showing us pictures of Bobbette." He pulled out his phone, swiping through his texts. "He sent me another one today. They're on their ranch in Culpepper, Wyoming this week, and Bobbette is crawling everywhere."

"Bobbette?" Michelle shook her head. "Please tell me that's a joke and just what people call her because her dad's name is Bob."

"I wish. Nope. May told him she was sick of naming characters in books, so he could name the baby whatever he wanted, and Bobbette is the result."

"That's awful!"

He shrugged. "It is, but it's not my kid, so I didn't get a voice in the name of the baby."

"I guess not. Does he know it's awful?"

"I really don't think so." He showed her the picture he found. "Isn't she darling?"

"She is!" Michelle leaned over to help with another trivia question.

Chapter Two

Steven was stiff when he woke the next morning, but he found the intense ache in his low back had lessened, and that's what he'd been after. He had an appointment with Dr. Michelle at eleven, and he'd be there, but he wouldn't be happy about it. He wanted her to see him once, fix him, and send him on his way. He understood that wasn't possible, but it still made him a bit crabby.

He decided to take a walk through the Old West town that morning and see what he could see. What little he'd seen of it the day before had fascinated him.

From what he'd been told, the inside of the buildings in the Old West town were mostly in use, but that wasn't a big deal. They could use the exteriors of some of the buildings, but use a studio for the interiors. If they worked with the ranch, they'd been promised a huge commissary for their employees' meals, and they'd said they'd work on other buildings as needed. Maybe they could build a set across the street for all the indoor shots.

As he looked around, he could almost see the series coming to life. He walked past an ancient tree in the center of the small town, and he smiled when he stopped at a pine tree in the middle. He had read about that tree in the book, and he would need to find a small one to showcase it better. Maybe it would be possible to start with a two-hour series premiere that would be exactly what the book was about, and after that, they could build the town around the people mentioned in the book.

The possibilities were endless, and this ranch seemed like exactly what he was looking for. He thought about going to talk to Wade—the brother he was told was the general manager of the ranch—before lunch, but he had to meet with Dr. Michelle. He groaned. She'd hurt him when she'd manipulated him, but he had to admit, he did feel significantly better today.

He walked toward the spa, all but dragging his feet, because he had no desire to go. And Dr. Michelle was so peppy when she talked to him. He kind of wanted to kick her, but didn't think it would be appropriate. Besides, she was a beautiful woman. He wondered what her policy was about dating a patient. They'd gone out the night before, but that had been different.

When he got to her office, she was waiting for him. "I have some physical therapy to start you on today. You're going to *love* this!"

She had him on his stomach, clenching his thighs and bottom, and rolling to his back and doing something she called dead bug. Was very annoying, but then she adjusted him.

"Tomorrow," she told him at the end of the visit.

He groaned. "I think I should have a day or two off, don't you?"

"Nope. You only have a week left, and I can tell you're the kind of person who wouldn't seek out a chiropractor at home, so I'm going to do as much good for you while you're here as I possibly can."

"Fine." He walked toward the door, turning around at the last minute. "Are you allowed to have lunch with patients?"

Dr. Michelle shrugged. "I had dinner with you last night, and lunch isn't that much different. It's still food, and you're still slowly shoveling sustenance into your mouth."

"Why don't you have lunch with me, then? I'm going to try Kelsi's Kafé, because I've heard the cook is just amazing."

"Sure. Let me grab my stuff." She went to her office off the main room and grabbed her purse, her heart beating faster. Steven was pretty darn attractive, and if he was interested in her as well, then she was going to make the most of it. "Okay, I'm ready."

"Let's go." He led her out the door and to the stairs, and then they walked across the parking lot, heading for the diner. He'd looked at the map on her office wall so he'd be sure he knew which way. "Do you eat at the diner often?"

"Sure. Whenever I get a chance. Bob is an amazing cook, even though he's one of the most annoying human beings on the planet. His wife is newly pregnant, though, and hopefully fatherhood will mellow him out a bit."

They walked into the café, and the pretty blonde he recognized as Dani's sister led them to a table. "Drinks?" she asked.

"Just ice water," Dr. Michelle said.

He nodded. "Ice water for me, too."

"I'll be right back! Special today is chicken and dumplings. Bob's aren't quite spicy enough in my opinion, so if you need to borrow some spice, I always have some on hand!" Kelsi hurried away, and Dr. Michelle laughed softly.

"She really carries Cajun seasoning everywhere. I've seen her do it. You'd think her tongue would have burned off by now with as much as she adds, but she says it's the only way food tastes good to her."

"Do you know her well?" Steven asked, surprised at what a tight-knit family the entire ranch seemed like to him.

"Pretty well. I adjusted her a lot when she was pregnant. She was the happiest pregnant woman alive, but she was in quite a bit of pain. I worried about her."

He watched Kelsi for a moment. "She seems really nice."

"Oh, Kelsi is insane. You've never met anyone quite as crazy as she is."

Kelsi brought back their waters, put her hands on her hips, and glared at Michelle. "I'm not insane. I just believe that we should all be in touch with the nature of the area."

Michelle looked at Steven. "What she means is she thinks everyone should believe that Bigfoot will be found any moment, because that's what she believes."

"I'm Kelsi Clapper. I'm the youngest of the six Weston children who run the ranch. Have I met you yet?" Kelsi asked Steven, ignoring Dr. Michelle's statement completely.

"I don't think you have. I'm Steven Pickman."

"Seriously? You're one of the directors of *Lazy Love*! I never miss a show! When I was in the hospital having the babies, I made the nurses watch it with me. Not like I had to twist their arms or anything, because everyone loves *Lazy Love*!"

"Not everyone," he said, looking at Dr. Michelle. "There's someone at this table who isn't a fan, but she's only seen one episode."

"Dr. Michelle doesn't like *Lazy Love*?" Kelsi shook her head. "I thought you had good taste, but now I know better. You're crazy!"

Dr. Michelle shook her head. "I'm not crazy. I just haven't really given it a chance. I'll try it again, okay?"

"It's on Netflix, so just start from the beginning and go from there. If you don't get sucked in immediately and declare it the best show on television, I will still love you." Kelsi shook her head. "I still can't believe you don't watch *Lazy Love*. It's un-American!"

Michelle shook her head, feeling a bit like the victim of a witch hunt. "I'll have the chicken and dumplings."

"Seasoning?" Kelsi asked.

"Yeah, drop it off." Michelle wasn't sure she'd use it, but she wouldn't mind having the option.

Steven shrugged. "I'll have the same."

After Kelsi had hurried off, Michelle glared at Steven. "I can't believe you threw me under the bus with Kelsi. That woman is absolutely insane about *Lazy Love*, and she's going to hound me for the rest of my life about it."

"Unless you start watching it." He grinned at her. "Why don't you come over to my cabin tonight, and we'll watch it together. I can tell you all the fun behind the scenes stuff that no one knows."

"Very tempting..." Michelle mentally went through her plans for the evening. "I have plans to work out with a friend at four. I could grab Chinese from town and bring it over around five-thirty? We can watch this amazing show and eat Chinese take-out."

"I like this plan!" The more time he spent with her outside of her torture chamber, the more he really liked her. "I have a hot tub if you want to bring a swim suit."

She nodded. "I would never turn down the chance to get in a hot tub. Especially with as cold as it is outside. I love being toasty warm and staring at the snowy landscape. Which cabin are you in?"

"Bearfoot."

"I'll be there."

Kelsi brought their food, pulling a green cannister from her pocket and setting it on the table as well. "You chose well. Whatever Bob's special is makes the perfect meal. No one can cook quite like Bob, but we don't tell him, because we don't want his head to swell more than it already is!" She raised her voice for the last sentence, only to have Bob stick his head out of the kitchen.

"Just because Joni took off and moved to Texas so she could be married to that cowboy of hers, doesn't mean you get to yell about me having a swelled head!"

"Someone has to!" she yelled back. Kelsi looked so proud of herself after the exchange that Michelle was shaking her head.

Steven couldn't believe the two of them were behaving so unprofessionally, but no one else seemed to even notice. "I promise not to tell Bob his cooking is amazing."

Kelsi grinned. "You're a good man. And not only because you direct my favorite television show and have the ability to get me a signed poster with all the stars' autographs."

"I have a few in my cabin. I'll bring one before I leave." Steven wasn't the best at reading between the lines, but Kelsi wasn't exactly subtle about what she was after.

"I knew I liked you!" Kelsi hurried away to deal with another table.

Steven looked at Michelle. "Does she always have that much energy?"

"Yep. You should have seen her when she was pregnant. She was having twins, and she didn't tell anyone she was having two until she was in labor. So she's wandering around looking like she just swallowed something roughly the size of a beach ball, and she's grinning like a crazy woman. No one could keep up with her even then. In fact, she went into labor during a snow sculpting tournament that she was participating in. Well, no, that's not right. She was in labor before, but didn't *tell* anyone until her team won."

He laughed. "Sounds very much like the woman I just met. I guess I have to love that about her, don't I?"

"We all do. No choice at all." Michelle took a bite of the dumplings and added a bit of the seasoning. It only needed a touch of salt, in her opinion, but she knew it would make Kelsi happy. And though there was no real reason she wanted to keep the girl happy, she found she did. And she knew many other people were the same. Kelsi was a bit confounding, but she spread joy wherever she went. A happy Kelsi was good for everyone.

"Is it good?" Steven asked, toying with it with his spoon.

"Bob is incapable of making a bad meal. They should clone him, and send him out everywhere, because he's absolutely amazing."

"So why does he work in the diner and not in the restaurant?"

Michelle shrugged. "No clue. I guess the Westons want to keep up the quality here. Kelsi's grandmother started this place, and it meant a lot to her."

"I can see that."

As they ate, she told him some stories about funny things that had happened on the ranch and some of the strange people there.

He paid for lunch, ignoring her protests. As they walked out together, he said, "So I'll see you around five-thirty or six?"

"I'll be there." As she walked away, she had a little skip to her step. There was something special about the man, even if he had gotten her into trouble with Kelsi. She couldn't wait to spend more time with him to see what made him tick.

Steven watched her go, smiling to himself. He hoped to spend more time with her. Lots more time with her if at all possible. He turned and walked toward the main ranch building, because he'd heard that's where Wade's office was located.

He went to the main desk and asked for Wade. "I have some business to discuss with him."

"Is there something I can help you with?"

"No, I really do need Wade."

"All right. Let me see if he's available." The girl picked up her phone and punched a couple of numbers. "He'll be here in a moment."

When Wade Weston walked into the lobby of the hotel, Steven immediately recognized him as the man in charge. He stepped forward. "I'm Steven Pickman. We spoke on the phone a few weeks ago."

Wade offered a hand to shake. "Absolutely. Let's talk in my office. No one knows why you're here yet." He led him through the building and back to an area that was obviously not meant for guests. "How are you enjoying your stay so far?"

"Well, it was good until I fell off the side of one of your mountains yesterday, and your sister had to come rescue me."

"Oh no! Were you hurt?"

"I hurt my back some, but Dr. Michelle is fixing me up."

Wade smiled. "She's good at what she does."

"And very nice to look at!"

"I'm glad you approve of the scenery around here." He opened the door to a small office. "Have a seat."

Steven took the chair facing the desk. "I think we want to do business with the ranch. We'll need a few things though."

Wade nodded. "I expected you would. I know we already talked about adding a commissary for your cast and crew. What else?" He picked up a pen, preparing to make notes of everything the man was looking for.

"I think the buildings in your Old West town will work perfectly for the outside shots, but we're going to need a studio of some sort that we can film the inside stuff in. Can you maybe make that happen across the street? Someone told me that land belongs to your family as well."

"Yes, I can absolutely do that. We'll also have a special area across the street for cast trailers."

"Sounds good. It might be good to create an apartment complex across the street, or extended stay hotel rooms with kitchens. Our stars like their comfort. Some would be willing to live in the trailers across from the set, but not all will. You could make some extra money that way and not lose it to people who would be willing to accommodate them in Riston."

Wade made a note. "I'm not sure if you realize that our ranch is actually owned by my siblings and me. I'll need to have a meeting with the whole group of them to discuss before any final decisions are made."

"Works for me."

"We'd also want to have the town only blocked off a couple of days per week. Will that work for you? So all outside shots would need to be done on say Tuesday and Thursday? Then the rest of the week, we can use our town as usual. We have a day care, an infirmary, a bakery, an art gallery, a bookstore, and so much more in the Old West town. We'd need to be sure we could keep up business as usual around here."

Steven nodded, thinking about it. "I really believe we could work around that. We'll need to do a series pilot, so a two-hour movie to sell the show to a network. If your family is willing to go forward with this, we'd want to start filming next month. The two-hour pilot would take about three weeks to film, and then it would be a while before we had an answer about whether the show's been picked up. I would say plan to accommodate fifty people starting on February first, and if we get picked up, you'll have about six months to get all the buildings we need done. During that time, we'll be in and out, making sure everything is to our specifications and will work for us."

Wade made more notes. "I'll call a meeting of my siblings later today, and I'll let you know within the next few days what we've decided. You still have a little longer here on the ranch, don't you?"

Steven nodded. "I have until Monday of next week. My partners and I love the idea of filming the show in the spot where the real event that sparked the book happened."

Wade nodded. "I don't think any of us realized that Kaya's book would get so much attention."

"The story just grabbed me and made me think that I'd love to bring it to life onscreen. I appreciate you being willing to work with us to make that happen."

"Absolutely. We love the idea, as long as our day-to-day operations aren't interrupted. We have a reputation for going all-out for our guests, and we want to keep that reputation. Of course, if they have the opportunity to be part of a television show as an extra, that would go really far with them. And with us."

Steven grinned. "There are always plenty of opportunities for extras. I'll make sure we broadcast among the guests first. I can't guarantee that we'll choose any specific person, but we will try to be very accommodating. We're prepared to offer you a good amount of money to make this idea a reality." He named a figure that had Wade's eyes widening.

Wade got to his feet, offering his hand to shake again. "I'll have an answer for you before you leave the ranch. I hope you have a good stay here."

"I certainly do enjoy the...scenery."

"Glad to hear it! Let me know if there's anything else I can do for you."

"Don't worry, I will." As Steven left the main house, he thought about how very much he wanted to do business with the ranch. He wasn't quite sure if it was because he loved the ranch so much, or because he wanted to spend more time with Dr. Michelle.

Chapter Three

While she was working out, Michelle couldn't help but wonder what had made her accept Steven's offer. She'd never gone out with a guest of the ranch or a patient...and he was both! She was certain she'd lost her mind.

But then she remembered how handsome he was. She had no idea why he'd gone into directing and not acting himself. No, she'd see him.

After her workout, she availed herself of the showers at the gym, which she hated doing. She didn't want to show up at his place feeling gross, though. She was getting in over her head, and she still wasn't sure if that was good or bad.

She went to the Chinese place and took Lin's suggestion, choosing three different meals to share, not sure what he liked. If he was picky, he should have told her, but she wanted to give him choices anyway.

When she pulled up in front of the Bearfoot Cabin, he opened the door immediately. He'd been watching for her, which thrilled her to no end. If she had to be sinking into the ocean of feelings, then he needed to be right along with her, fighting to tread water.

Getting out of the car, Michelle held up the Chinese, and he hurried to take it from her. "Did you do your exercises?" she asked.

"Yes, I did, and no more being a doctor. Tonight, we're just watching television together, and you're not being bossy Dr. Michelle."

She frowned for a moment. "I'm not sure if I know how to be anything *but* bossy." She'd been called bossy more times than she could count, but she didn't worry about it. If a man was intimidated by a strong woman, then he wasn't the man for her anyway.

He shook his head, setting the food on the counter and walking over to get out plates. "I'm sure you can figure it out if you try hard enough."

"I'll get right on that." She watched him as he put plates and serving spoons as well as a couple of forks on the counter. "I got chopsticks."

He shrugged. "We can fence with them later. I prefer forks."

"All right." She filled her plate and grabbed a fork. "Are we eating at the table?"

He shook his head. "Nah. I thought we could eat in front of the television. You're here to see my show."

She nodded. "I am." She took her plate into the living room and set it on the coffee table, dropping to the floor in front of it. She couldn't believe how different they were about just about everything. Eating at a table was important to her, so she'd eat at the coffee table, and he could do whatever he liked.

He sat down on the couch, frowning at her. Why on earth was the woman on the floor? He certainly couldn't get down there right now. Was she trying to avoid him? Strange. He picked up the remote control, flipped the television to Netflix, and started with the first episode. "Which episode did you see?"

She shrugged. "I'm not sure. I was at a friend's house, and it was on."

That explained a lot to him. Most television shows needed to be watched in order to be understood, and Lazy Love was no exception. He pushed play and watched as the opening credits scrolled. The four main actors all stood with their arms crossed and they flipped from one to the next. "That's Valerie. She plays Jo. That's Jesse. He plays Dylan."

She nodded, not sure why he was telling her all this. Maybe if she understood what was happening she'd like it better, though. Shoving a big piece of sweet and sour chicken into her mouth, she paid attention to the screen.

"That's Bob. He plays Bob. And that's Amber, the star who plays MaryBeth."

It didn't take long for her to be sucked into the first episode, which was a two-hour pilot. She watched as the hero and heroine of the show met for the first time. She wanted to cheer for them to start kissing, but she was sure Steven would let it go to his head, so she watched calmly.

As soon as it was over, she turned to Steven. "Not nearly as bad as I thought it was."

"It makes a lot more sense if you watch it in order. Our writers do a great job on the show."

"Am I right in thinking that the girl who plays Jo is now married to the man who plays Dylan?"

"Yep. And they're expecting their second child. That's not public knowledge yet though. She just found out. We're having to start later in the day at the moment, because she doesn't feel well in the mornings. It's a good thing we're ahead of schedule. Of course, when I'm in charge of a project we're always ahead of schedule. Just flying in under the wire by the seat of our pants doesn't particularly work for me."

She grinned. "I can agree with that philosophy!" She tilted her head to one side, thinking about it. "That may be the first thing we've agreed on."

Steven laughed. "Maybe it is. I'm not even sure. It's nice to agree though, isn't it?"

Michelle shrugged. "I'm going to put my dishes in the sink before we start the next one. Do you want a fortune cookie while I'm up?"

"Yeah, that'd be great."

She took his plate and put them both in the sink. For a moment she thought about washing them, but she didn't want to start any bad habits. If they were going to have a relationship—and at the moment she had no idea how they would—then she would not be doing *all* the dishes. It would need to be more of an equitable division of labor. She worked, too.

She took back two fortune cookies, handing him one and keeping one for herself. Cracking her cookie, she pulled out the fortune. "Listen to the fairies. They're always right." She blinked at it for a moment, and shook her head. Did that mean Jaclyn was going to involve herself in her life? The older woman who—along with her gnomes, fairies, and snickerdoodles was a permanent part of the ranch—tended to meddle in everyone's love lives, claiming she was told by the fairies what to do.

"What does yours say?" Michelle asked, curious if the local Chinese place had started putting in fortunes about fairies to mess with people's heads. Surely, they knew about Jaclyn and her fairies. Everyone did. It would be just like Jaclyn to talk them into doing something like that.

Steven frowned at the words in his hand. "It says, 'The fairies know—even if you don't.' That doesn't make any sense." He read it three more times before he put it down, chalking it up to a crazy person writing his fortune.

She sighed. "I think the people at the Chinese restaurant had special fortunes made to mess with our heads. And by 'our' I mean all the people on the ranch."

"That doesn't make a lot more sense to me than the fortune. What does it mean?" Had she suddenly lost her mind when she read her fortune?

She grinned. "I forget that everyone doesn't know about Jaclyn. She's this older woman who does her best to match everyone on the ranch up with each other. She claims the fairies guide her, telling her what to say to people. If you see a house with gnomes and fairies on the lawn, don't go up to it!"

"Are you afraid she'd try to hook us up romantically?" he asked, wondering what would be so wrong about that. He liked the idea of more coming from their friendship.

She sighed. "You know, if we do it ourselves, it's one thing. If people try to push us together, it's something else entirely."

He nodded. "I guess I can understand that." Wanting to make a move, he wasn't sure he should after what she'd said. "Want to watch the next one?"

"Yeah, I think I'm starting to see the appeal." Michelle settled onto the couch beside him, not too close, but not exactly far away from him either.

Steven held up the remote and started the show, his mind still thinking about the whole fairy thing. He'd go see the woman the next day. Why not? The only other thing he needed to do was let the leggy woman sitting beside him abuse him.

They watched two more shows before she stood and stretched. "I have to sleep if I'm going to be able to see patients tomorrow."

He got to his feet. "All right. I'll see you at the office. Thanks for giving my show a chance."

"I really did like it. Now I'm going to have to watch it whenever I've got a few minutes." Though she didn't really need another distraction in her life.

"Sounds good to me. And you could always come back tomorrow to watch more."

Michelle had never been one to beat around the bush, so she turned to face him, her eyes meeting his. "Are you trying to start something with me?" she asked.

Steven took a step closer to her. "Even though you and I don't seem to see eye-to-eye on much of anything, I'm very attracted to you."

"Really? Good." She stepped closer to him and wound her arms around his back, pressing her lips to his. As first kisses went, it rated right up there with Jimmy Reynolds, her first boyfriend in tenth grade. He'd kissed her and she'd seen fireworks. With Steven it was more like rockets, but same general idea.

Steven grinned at her. "That's what I've been trying to get up the guts to do all night." He couldn't believe she'd just grabbed him and kissed him. He liked her a little more every minute!

"Guts? With me? I'm very much a plain-spoken, call it as I see it kind of girl. If I want something, I do it. Next time just grab me and kiss me. I'll respect you a lot more for it."

He grabbed her shoulders and pulled her back to him, kissing her once more. This time, he deepened the kiss as he stood with her, locking her against him. "Goodnight, Michelle."

She was slightly out of breath as she looked at him through her wide eyes. "Goodnight, Steven."

He stepped outside with her. "Do you live here on the ranch?"

She shook her head. "No, I live in a duplex in town. I didn't want to live where I worked. Some do, but it would just be a bit weird to me."

He walked her over to her car and closed the door after she got in. He stood there and waved goodbye, before turning to go back into the cabin.

"Do you believe in fairies?" a voice asked from behind him.

He turned, wondering if this was the woman he'd been warned about. He was already fascinated by her. "I'm not sure, but I'm certainly open to the idea of them. Why not?" He couldn't quite see her in the dark, but he knew it had to be her.

She stepped out into the driveway and under a lamp. She was wearing a thick, heavy winter coat and had a rabbit on a leash. "I'm Jaclyn."

"It's nice to meet you Jaclyn. Would you like to come inside?" He had a lot of questions he wanted to ask her, and he didn't particularly want to stand out in the snow to ask them all.

Jaclyn shook her head. "No, but I'd like it if you came to my house tomorrow. At three in the afternoon. I'll serve tea and snickerdoodles. That won't interfere with your appointment with Dr. Michelle, will it?"

He shook his head. "Not at all. I'll see her right before lunch." He didn't even think to question her knowing about his appointment with Dr. Michelle. He was sure it wasn't every day someone fell off the mountain.

Jaclyn smiled with a nod. "Good. I hope you feel better soon. Falling off the mountain is never the smartest way to meet a woman, but it does seem to be working for you." With that, she was gone, and Steven stood staring at the spot where she'd just been.

Steven walked back into the house, wondering about the woman he'd just met. She was certainly a bit eccentric, but he didn't dismiss the paranormal. Living in California had taught him that anything was possible.

STEVEN TALKED MICHELLE into lunch again the next day. "So should we eat at the diner again? Or should we go somewhere in town?" he asked.

"We won't find food that even begins to compare to the diner's anywhere in town. Diner is always the best bet if it's open." Michelle locked the door to her small office and turned to him. "So let's go see what Bob's special is today."

"What if I don't want to get the special, and instead I get something wild and crazy? Like an omelet?"

She shrugged. "Whatever floats your boat. If you don't want to eat the special that's up to you. I've had everything on the menu, and I just know that if I have the special every day, I can't go wrong." He could be wrong and get something else. No skin off her nose.

For a moment, he thought about telling her he'd met Jaclyn the night before, but he decided against it. "How long have you been working on the ranch?"

"About eighteen months. I love it here. The fresh air is worth all of the inconveniences of living so rurally."

"Are you into all the woowoo medicine stuff?" he asked.

"I don't know what you consider woowoo, but I like to use alternative medicine before turning to Western medicine most of the time. If I had cancer, I think I'd go see a medical doctor. If I had diabetes, I'd probably see a medical doctor. I think most things can be fixed with a balanced diet and herbal remedies, though."

He considered her answer for a moment, but he realized he agreed with most of what she said. She wasn't overboard into the alternative stuff. "If I came to you with a bleeding ulcer, what would you do?"

"I'd send you to a doctor who could deal with your ailment. I'm not crazy. I'd probably tell you to fix your diet and reduce your stress first, though."

They got to the diner, and he opened the door. Michelle caught Kelsi's eyes and nodded to the same booth they'd been in the day before. Kelsi nodded back, hiding a yawn. As soon as they were seated, Kelsi stuck menus in front of them. "Special today is pot roast, mashed potatoes, and green beans. He's also including some hot dinner rolls fresh from the bakery."

"Oh, that sounds great." Dr. Michelle didn't bother to look at her menu. She knew that would make her happy. "And ice water."

"Yup." Kelsi looked at Steven. "You know what you want yet?"

"I think I want a minute to look at the menu."

"Water again?"

"Yes, please."

"All right. I'll be back in a minute with your drinks." Kelsi wandered off toward the kitchen to put their orders in.

"She looks really tired," Michelle said, frowning after her. "I wonder if the babies are keeping her up."

"Isn't that what babies do?" he asked, not terribly concerned. Of course, he didn't know Kelsi like she did. He understood that she worried about all of her patients, and he was sure that in her place, he'd feel the same.

"Yeah, but she usually has her mother here helping out some, and her assistant manager just got married and moved off." Michelle decided she'd talk to one of the other Westons and ask them to keep an eye on Kelsi for a while. She was worried about her.

"Sounds like she needs a new assistant manager. There have to be people around willing to take the job."

"Yeah. Probably." Michelle picked up her phone and checked her email really quickly, tapping a response to her brother, who was dating a good friend of hers.

"I think I know what I want." Steven closed his menu.

"What are you getting?" she asked.

"The Western Burger. Is it any good?" he asked.

"If I'm in the mood for a burger, that's the only one that will satisfy me." Michelle shrugged. "If you're not going to have the daily special—and I still think you should—the Western Burger is a good alternative." She really had a hard time with him playing willy nilly with the menu, getting whatever he wanted. That wasn't the special!

"Then I'll have that."

"Oh, and we should get fried cheese curds. Bob makes this special sauce to dip them in, and it's just amazing."

"That sound good. With all those exercises you're making me do, I'm burning a lot more calories than usual." Besides, he had to walk around and find Jaclyn's house later. He couldn't help but wonder what the woman wanted from him. She seemed a bit daffy, but he'd met much worse.

"Exercise is good for you. I still work out every day."

"What time are you working out tonight?" he asked, determined to lure her back to his cabin for more *Lazy Love*. He wanted her to be as invested in the show as he was.

"I went this morning before work. Sometimes I even work out between patients. It gives me something to do with my time."

"Do you really need something to do? You seem to always be busy."

She shrugged. "If I'm not seeing patients, I'm doing something. I refuse to let my brain atrophy."

"Makes sense."

Kelsi wandered over with their water then. "Know what you want?" she asked Steven. She was one of the most casual waitresses he'd ever met, and he loved how easy she was to deal with.

"We were just talking, and we want to share the cheese curds, and I want a Western Burger."

"Good choice." Kelsi scribbled on a note pad. "You need root beer with the cheese curds, though. I promise you, nothing tastes as good as cheese curds and root beer."

Steven shrugged. "All right. Bring me a root beer then."

"Me too," Michelle said. She didn't normally drink pop, but it sounded wonderful right at that moment.

"All right. Back in a few."

"How long do you have for lunch?" Steven asked her.

She shrugged. "My next appointment is at one. I can take that long if I want. I usually just take an hour, but sometimes I take longer."

"Do you want to walk over to the Old West town with me after? There's some stuff I want to look at." He wasn't going to tell her his real purpose there until he heard back from Wade, but he did need some more time looking around the area. And if it meant more time with her...well, he'd jump at a chance to spend time with her.

"Sure."

Kelsi hurried over. "I almost forgot to ask if you converted Dr. Michelle to a lover of *Lazy Love*."

Michelle grinned. "I understand the appeal. I'm not quite as addicted as you are, but I think after a few more shows, I just might be."

Kelsi grinned, her blue eyes sparkling. "Sounds wonderful. Keep working on her!" She hurried away again, a spring in her step.

Chapter Four

As they walked through the Old West town, Steven peppered Michelle with questions. "Do you know if these buildings are authentic or if they were built to look authentic?"

Michelle shrugged. "Some of each, I think. I'm not sure which is which, but any Weston could tell you."

"I never seem to see people walking around in this area. Is it popular?"

"Yeah, it is. This is one of the quietest weeks of the year. Kids are just getting back to school and parents don't want to pull them out. In a couple of weeks, the whole ranch will be bustling again. You'd be surprised at how busy the ranch stays year-round. There's fun stuff to do all the time."

"Like fall off the mountain?"

Michelle shook her head at him. "Most people wouldn't include that in the fun stuff available on the ranch. Trust you to think of things differently..."

He grinned. "What's this building." He knew that all of the shops in the town were covers for something else.

"This is a bakery." She looked at him as if he'd lost his mind.

"I know it says bakery, but what is it really."

"A bakery! Bob's wife Miranda works here. She's amazing." Michelle took his hand and tugged him inside. "Hey, Miranda! This is Steven. He was trying to figure out what the bakery really was."

Miranda grinned. "It's really a bakery. I baked some new cookies today. Care to sample?" She held a tray over the counter toward them.

Michelle grabbed a piece and popped it in her mouth, not even bothering to ask what kind it was. She knew if Miranda made it, it was delicious. "Oh, that's wonderful! What is it?"

"Well, I've been playing with gingersnaps, and I added some caramel bits to these. You really like it?"

"I love it! In fact, I need to buy three." Michelle wanted half a dozen, but she'd buy three, and give one to Steven. She couldn't justify eating six, and she didn't want to have to spend all of her time working off the calories.

"Works for me!" Miranda efficiently put the cookies into a bag and handed it over the display case. "Anything else?"

"Just a bottle of water." Michelle looked at Steven. "Do you want water with your cookie?"

"One of those is for me?" He was a bit surprised, because she hadn't seemed to want to share.

"Yes, but just one. Water?"

"Yes, please."

Miranda handed them two bottles of water, and Michelle paid, elbowing Steven when he reached for his wallet. "How are you feeling? Morning sickness kicking your butt?"

Miranda grinned. "This is the first week I haven't been sick. I'm at twelve weeks now, and it seems to be easier."

"I bet your mom is ecstatic about being a grandmother."

"Yes! She comes in every day to make sure I'm feeling all right. She's lost her mind! Frank needs to do something to distract her."

Michelle laughed. "Well, you look wonderful. I'm glad you're feeling better." She took her change, waving as she opened the door to go back outside. Opening the bag, she handed one cookie to Steven. "I'm glad you asked, because these cookies are to die for."

He shook his head. "You're crazy. Okay, let's look down here. The saloon? That's not really a saloon?"

"Nah. That's a soda shop. Sadie does homemade ice cream that's to die for. She also does specialty coffees. Definitely worth stopping in if you ever have the time." She glanced at the time on her phone. "But I don't. I need to get back to the office."

"Will I see you tonight?"

She grinned. "I get off at four. Do you want to eat at the restaurant? Or we can go into town?"

"I'll cook."

She raised an eyebrow. "You cook? Really?"

"I do, but don't run around telling people. I don't want them to think I need to cook for them, because...not happening."

She laughed. "All right. I'll see you after work. Are we doing another *Lazy Love* marathon?"

"Sure. I don't know why not."

She rushed off toward the office, her long-legged strides eating up the ground in front of her. She was a no-nonsense determined woman. Steven liked that about her.

As soon as she was out of sight, he dialed Wade's number. "Wade, it's Steven. Any news for me?"

"We're getting together this evening. We usually only meet on Sundays, so everyone thinks something crazy is going on. I'll have something to tell you tomorrow."

"Sounds good to me." He ended the call and walked slowly toward the lake. He loved having a cabin right on it, and he found himself watching the water often. He did it from the comfort of his bedroom, because it was awfully cold out, but he still did it. California boys were not made for cold weather like this. Of course, he'd been raised in Massachusetts, so it wasn't all that unusual for him. He still liked to watch the cold from in front of a roaring fire, though.

As he walked, he munched on his cookie and drank his water, wondering where Jaclyn's house was. From Michelle's description, he was certain there was no way he could miss it, so he kept an eye out as he walked.

He still had an hour before he was supposed to be there, but he had a feeling that Jaclyn was not someone you should keep waiting.

He stopped in front of a house, smiling to himself. *This must be it. I can see the mounds of statues under the snow.*

Jaclyn stepped out onto the porch. "Well, come on! The fairies said you were going to be ridiculously early, and they were right. I have the cookies and tea waiting for you."

"I was just making sure I could find it so I wouldn't be late. I'll come back!"

"And make me heat up more water for tea? That would be rude!" Jaclyn shook her head at him. "You don't strike me as a rude boy."

"I—" He stopped talking. He could tell he was just going to dig a hole for himself, and his actor friend Bob liked to tell him that when he was in a hole, he needed to stop digging. Steven walked slowly toward her house, a bit nervous about what to expect.

"Get in here! It's cold out. Do you not have the sense God gave a gnat? Why are you standing out there in the cold when there's hot tea waiting for you inside?"

He didn't respond, and instead walked into the house. Surely, she was going to tell him something helpful, or she wouldn't have called him there.

"Sit down!" she insisted, waving her hand toward a couch that seemed to be completely covered in bunnies. How many rabbits could one woman have?

He picked one up and put it on the floor, taking its spot. It was nice to sit for a moment, because his back was aching again. He'd have to do more of the exercises Michelle swore by before he saw her. He didn't mind working out, but her exercises just made him grumpy.

"Well? Don't you have anything to say?" Jaclyn asked.

"I had a strange fortune in my cookie last night when we ate Chinese food. It said, 'The fairies know—even if you don't.' Does that mean anything to you?"

Jaclyn cackled. "It means they're tormenting you. What have you done to deserve that?"

"Nothing that I know of. What could I have done to make fairies angry?"

She studied him for a moment, as if trying to figure out exactly what it all meant. "Why are you here on the ranch?" she finally asked.

He frowned. "I can't tell you that until I know what's going to come of my visit."

"But you're not a regular guest, are you? The fairies think you're trying to change the ranch. Are you trying to change their home?"

"Not really. I'm going to do everything I can *not* to change it." He accepted the cup of tea she offered and a small plate with two cookies on it. "I was hoping you were going to give me advice about Dr. Michelle."

Jaclyn grinned, her teeth bared. "Are you having trouble with her?"

"I wouldn't say trouble. I just feel really strongly for her, and I've only known her for a couple of days, so that's strange for me." He had never in his life felt such an immediate affinity to a woman. He had no idea what was wrong with him.

"Are you sure they're real feelings, and it's not just because she treated you? Isn't there a name for falling in love with your doctor?"

He frowned. "I don't think that's what it is..."

She laughed hysterically. "I was just trying to mess with your head. You're an easy victim!"

"So you don't have advice for me about her?"

"Sure I do. I have a message from the fairies, but they want to know what you're doing here, too. You'd think they'd know because they know every other dang thing." She shook her head. "One of them moved Gorgeous George from his normal spot to another under a different tree. Someone said it was probably kids, but kids wouldn't be able to move him without disturbing the snow at all, would they?"

"I wouldn't think so..." Steven wondered if she was ever going to get back to the message the fairies had for him, but he wasn't sure what she'd do if he asked.

"Oh, I know you don't want to hear about how the fairies are fighting with the gnomes again. No one wants to listen to that. They just want me to give them the messages the fairies have for them. Well, fine. Here's your message. 'You don't have to fall off a mountain to get her attention. Be careful.' Happy now?"

He frowned. "I wasn't planning on falling off a mountain again. Once in a lifetime is more than enough for me."

"Good, because when the fairies told me you did that just to meet Dr. Michelle, I thought you were daft!"

"I didn't do it just to meet her. It was an accident." How could he have deliberately fallen off a mountain to meet a woman he had no idea existed?

"Did you or did you not fall off the mountain?"

"I did."

"And then a couple of hours later, you were with Dr. Michelle and she was fixing you up, right?"

"Yes, but—"

"No buts. You fell off the mountain so you could meet a beautiful woman, and while I have to applaud your ingenuity, it was a bit stupid to actually hurt yourself in the process." Jaclyn shook her head. "Don't you think you should have just pretended to fall? That would have been smarter."

He closed his eyes, realizing the conversation was going in circles, and he was never going to convince her he hadn't deliberately fallen off the mountain. In a way, she reminded him of his grandmother, and he suddenly felt the urge to help her. "Is there anything I can do while I'm here?"

"What do you mean by that?" she asked, surprised.

"I thought maybe there were some chores I could take care of for you. I could shovel the front walk or something."

"You can't shovel after hurting your back throwing yourself down the mountain. That wouldn't be smart at all!" Jaclyn smiled at him, surprising him a little. "I do have a light out in my bathroom I could use help with, though. Could you help with that?"

"Yes, ma'am. I'd be happy to!" He got to his feet, and she showed him where the lightbulbs were and which light was out.

When he was finished with the task, he handed her the burnt-out bulb. "Anything else I can do?"

"Not that I can think of. Well, you can stop falling off mountains, but I think we've already beaten that horse to death."

He grinned, enjoying her colorful speech. She made him wish he was a writer, so he could capture her on the page. He wondered if he'd be able to talk her into being an extra. Of course, she'd have to leave the bunnies at home...he wasn't sure it was possible.

"Thank you for the tea, cookies, and advice. I had a wonderful time." He leaned down and brushed his lips across her cheek. "I'll visit you again before I have to leave."

She frowned at him. "I was really hoping we could keep you. When do you leave?"

"Monday, but I have this strange feeling I'll be back."

"Are you going to take Dr. Michelle off with you when you go?"

"I don't think so. She seems really happy here."

"She wouldn't be without you." Jaclyn frowned at him. "I hope you're listening, boy, because the fairies know you two shouldn't be split up!"

"I'm listening to every word." He walked toward the door, feeling too big for the small house that seemed to hold the entire rabbit population of Idaho. "Thank you again for the wonderful snack."

Jaclyn walked to the door and watched him leave. He knew because he turned around and waved at her. She was a special lady, and he hoped everyone on the ranch valued her. She deserved it.

His next stop was the general store, where he needed to pick up some groceries so he could fix supper for Michelle. The fruit basket the ranch had provided upon his arrival just wasn't sufficient for a good meal.

He went in and looked at the small grocery case and the one shelf with staples. He still had a little while, and though the store had a good selection, he wanted to have more choices.

"May I help you?" a young woman asked.

"Yes, I'm looking for a more extensive selection of food than what you have available here. Where's the closest grocery store?"

"Riston. It's about a twenty-minute drive."

He frowned. "I think I can make it there and back before my date joins me for supper. Can you give me directions?" He'd been flown onto the ranch by the resident pilot, Frank, and he hadn't left since his arrival.

"Oh, absolutely. Let me just draw you a map. Once you see it in black and white, it's easy. Really only two turns to town and the grocery store is on the main road." She quickly scribbled a map out and handed it to him.

"Thank you so much." The girl was dressed in clothes that looked authentic to the period the show would take place in. He hoped they could use her as an extra. "What's your name?"

"Heidi."

"Thank you, Heidi. I really appreciate your help." He hurried from the store, half-running back to his car. He was still a little sore from his fall, and he had plenty of bruises, but his back was healing nicely. Michelle may be a bit rough with her adjustments, but she really did seem to know her stuff.

An hour later, he was in the kitchen of the cabin, his groceries spread out around him. He was a good cook, but he was also a messy cook. He promised himself to clean as he went this time, because he didn't want his cabin to be a wreck when Michelle arrived.

Once the chicken was in the oven and the potatoes were boiling, he mixed a salad. He didn't know what she liked in her salad, but he was very much a kitchen sink salad maker. Everything he could think of was tossed in there, making it more fun and enjoyable to eat.

He found a tablecloth in one of the kitchen drawers, and he spread it out over the table, adding a candle he'd purchased to the middle of the table.

When all was said and done, the table looked perfect. He hurried into the kitchen and loaded the dishwasher with the dishes he'd used, wiping off the counters. Just as he was taking the meat out of the oven, there was a knock on the door, and he hurried over to open it. "You're right on time."

Michelle walked in, sniffing deeply. "That smells delicious!"

"I thought since we had beef for lunch, I'd do chicken for supper. We have salad, chicken, and potatoes." He was proud of how clean he'd gotten the kitchen after his cooking spree.

She took her coat off, hanging it on a hook beside the front door. "I can't wait to try it. If I can judge by the smell, you could give Bob a run for his money."

"I could, but I couldn't cook so many different things all at once. Everyone would have to eat whatever I made, and I would need three or four sous chefs to clean up the mess I made."

She grinned at that. "Well, I don't think I could cook this well, with or without sous chefs. I'm excited to try it."

He waved her away from the kitchen. "Go wait at the table. I'll serve you."

"I could get used to this, you know." She walked to the table and sat down at one of places he'd set.

He brought the salad first, and she was amazed at all of the things he'd thought to put into it. As soon as he was sitting, she tried a bite. "This is wonderful."

"It's just a salad. Wait until you try the main course."

She grinned at him, impressed that he could not only cook, but he was willing to do so. So many men weren't willing to work in a kitchen to please a woman. She was very happy with him at that moment.

Chapter Five

Steven and Michelle watched another three episodes of *Lazy Love* that night, before she called a halt to the evening. She turned to him on the couch after the third episode. "I'm exhausted. I'm not used to being out late."

"I just want to spend every minute I can with you before I leave. It's already Wednesday, and I need to leave Monday."

She sighed. "I wish I could just take off for a week, but I can't. I can spend the weekend with you."

"I'd like that a lot." He reached out and drew her closer, his lips meeting hers. "How did I get so attached to a *chiropractor* that I've only known for two days?"

"You say chiropractor like it's a dirty word. Your back is already doing better!"

He grinned at that. "It is doing better. Of course, I'll never admit in public that I've seen a quack."

"Just call me a duck, would you?" She got to her feet, stretching. She wasn't used to sitting still for the length of three one-hour episodes. "Do you want my help with the dishes before I go?"

He shook his head. "Nope. I'll cram them all in the dishwasher before bed. No big deal." He stood up and pulled her to him for one last kiss of the night. "Lunch again tomorrow?"

She nodded. "Absolutely. And I'm seeing you in my office at eleven, right?"

He wrinkled his nose. "If you weren't helping me, I wouldn't keep coming back."

She patted his arm affectionately. "No one would." Kissing his cheek quickly, she hurried out the door to her car. It was so hard to leave him every night. She was losing her mind just for thinking it, but she was pretty sure she was falling in love. With a man who would be out of her life in five days. What on earth was she thinking?

"You're thinking he's a good man who is good for you. That's what you're thinking."

Michele almost groaned. She knew that voice. "Hi, Jaclyn."

"You know avoiding me isn't going to keep you from falling for him, right?"

"Obviously not." Michelle lifted her head high. "I think it's too late anyway. He's going back to Texas soon, with my heart in his pocket."

"Well, have you told him?" Jaclyn asked, her usual blunt self.

Michelle shook her head. "I've barely admitted it to myself. Give me a few days to freak out, and then I'll move on!"

"Don't freak out. He's a good man. He changed my light bulb when he came for tea today."

"Wait...I told him to avoid you. Why did he come for tea?"

"Because he's a polite young man, and I invited him. I think I remind him of his grandmother or something, because after tea, he asked what chores he could do for me. He's a *very* good man."

"That was really sweet of him, but...I don't want anyone to try and match us up." Michelle hated the idea of something trying to force the two of them together.

"I don't need to match you. You've done that yourselves. I'm just trying to make sure the two of you don't overlook the obvious and go your separate ways because you're both lunkheads."

Michelle sighed. "I'll do my best not to be a lunkhead."

"It may not be easy. Lunkheadedness is innate. It's not something you can easily fix, I'm afraid!"

Michelle opened the door to her car, eyeing Jaclyn. "I promise we'll both do our best." *Now stay out of it!*

"Don't let him leave here without knowing how you feel, all right?"

Michelle shrugged. She'd make no such promise. She couldn't put her heart on the line with a man she barely knew. "We'll see."

"Lunkhead." Jaclyn turned away and disappeared into the night, leaving Michelle trying not to laugh.

Michelle had never been called a lunkhead before, and now it was several times in one night. She had no idea what a lunkhead was, but she'd try not to be one!

On her drive home, she thought about what Jaclyn had said. She didn't want to feel like a heroine in a movie who was dashing after a man who was leaving her forever, yelling, "I love you!" But she didn't want to jump the gun either. What if her feelings for him were just mutual attraction? She'd never been in love before, so how was she supposed to know what it felt like?

She fell asleep that night with visions of herself chasing his train down a track, yelling that she loved him over and over dancing through her mind. Jaclyn needed to leave them alone. There was no way she was ready to say those words to him yet. None.

DURING HIS WALK THE following morning, Steven got a call from Wade Weston. "This is Steven."

"Hey there. We're ready to talk money. And my youngest sister has a really weird stipulation, so if you want to head over here and talk to me, I'll tell you what it is."

Steven was definitely interested in what one of his sisters had to say. His youngest? Did that mean the crazy Kelsi? Or the delightful Dani? "I'll be there in a few. I'm walking through the Old West town now."

As he walked, he spotted Jaclyn with a man he didn't recognize. He couldn't help but wonder if they were sweethearts, to use an old-fashioned phrase. It looked like the man thought she hung the moon and stars, but Jaclyn didn't seem as interested in him. He knew looks of interest. He made actors give them to people they didn't care about all the time.

He hurried to the main house, his back better than it had been the day before. He hated the exercises and adjustments, but he was happy for the progress, so he couldn't complain too loudly. It's not like anyone would listen to him anyway. He'd found that people did their best to tune out complaints, but they really listened when there was something good to listen to.

When he reached the main house, he went back to Wade's office and stopped by the man's assistant. "May I help you?"

"Wade is expecting me. I'm Steven Pickman."

The woman nodded efficiently. "Yes, of course. Go right in."

Steven walked through the open door to Wade's office and closed it behind him, sitting down in the chair across from his desk. "What kind of demands?"

Wade laughed. "I figured that would intrigue you. Kelsi wants you to arrange for all of the stars of *Lazy Love* to come here and sign posters and meet the guests. I told her she was being unreasonable, but have you ever tried arguing with her? It was like talking to a wall!"

Steven grinned. "I can picture it." He thought for a moment. Could he get the cast there? It would have to be a paid venture, and he wasn't sure if anyone would go for it. "Let me make a few calls, and I'll see if I can make it happen. I'll meet with you tomorrow?"

"Absolutely. Oh, and one other demand."

"Kelsi again?"

Wade shook his head. "Nope. My brother Will wants you to audition our cousin. You don't have to cast her, but she's trying to get her big break in Hollywood, and the audition would help her."

"Sure. I can do that." Steven stood up. "I'll be back tomorrow with answers. Is this time all right?"

"Definitely." Wade stood and they shook hands. "You haven't even asked what we're going to ask you to pay us for the privilege of using our town."

"Have a contract drawn up for me tomorrow, and I'll look at the number then."

"Sounds good."

Steven let himself out of the office and walked toward the spa. He was ready to be manhandled—or was it womanhandled—by Michelle again. More than ready.

AFTER HIS ADJUSTMENT, Steven and Michelle went to the café again. "You'd think this was the only place that served food in all of Idaho!" he said.

Michelle shrugged. "I believe it's the best."

"It's got great food. I'll give you that." He opened the door for them, and they took the same spot as the last couple of days. Kelsi hurried over. "Two waters. Special today is a hearty beef stew. And there's a salad that comes with it. Back in a minute with the water."

"She's definitely efficient," Steven said to Michelle as Kelsi hurried away.

"Yup." Michelle pushed her menu to the middle of the table. "Are we doing cheese curds again?"

He nodded. "They were delicious. I can't believe I've lived my whole life without them."

"Do we need root beer then?"

"I think we do. I don't usually drink soft drinks, but Kelsi was right. They really are the perfect pairing with the cheese curds." He looked at his menu for a minute before closing it. "I enjoyed my burger yesterday, but the whole time I ate it, I kept looking at your special and wishing I'd gotten that instead. I'm sticking with the special today."

Michelle nodded at him. "Wise choice. I thought you were crazy for eating off the menu yesterday."

He reached for her hand across the table, threading his fingers through hers. "I should have listened to you. You are a very *wise* woman."

"It's about time you recognized that fact!" Michelle felt a flutter in her stomach as he took her hand in his. It was his first public display of affection, and she liked it more than she probably should.

"Are we watching the show tonight?"

Michelle shrugged. "I feel like we should do more than just watch television together. We should go for a sleigh ride. I think your back is up for it now, and they're a lot of fun."

"A sleigh ride, huh? I guess I could do that if you'll guarantee I won't fly out of the sleigh and break my butt."

"Well, I don't think you will, but can flying out of a sleigh be any worse than falling off a mountain? Really?"

Kelsi pushed their water in front of them, and they placed their order. Steven picked up something he'd been carrying around all morning and handed it to her.

Kelsi squealed as she took it, quickly unrolling it to see the signatures and faces of all the people from her favorite show. "I think I might just love you, Steven Pickman." She leaned down and kissed him on the top of his head.

From the next table over came a protest. "Kelsi? What have I told you about kissing other men when I'm right here?"

"He gave me a poster of the *Lazy Love* cast and their signatures! I had to kiss him, Shane! You understand."

The sheriff stood up and walked over to the table where Michelle sat with Steven. He was a big man, and more than a little bit intimidating. "Thanks for doing something nice for my wife."

Steven nodded. "Happy to do it. She's a dedicated viewer of the show I direct."

"Oh! You're the guy from *Lazy Love*. She's not a dedicated viewer. She's a certifiable freak who is looney tunes over the show. You might want a restraining order, and I can help you with that."

Kelsi laughed, putting her arm around Shane's waist. "You know you love me just as I am."

"I wouldn't change a hair on your head. Thank you for not naming my baby Widget."

She giggled. "I never would have, but it sure was fun watching you sweat."

Michelle grinned, remembering the fun they'd all had when Kelsi had been trying to decide on the right name for the baby. You never knew what was going to come out of her mouth next, but Widget had definitely been one of her favorites. "Do you ever call Willow Widget when no one's looking?"

Kelsi laughed. "Not often."

Shane shook his head, a look of love on his face visible through the very obvious exasperation. "No more!"

Kelsi stood on tiptoes and kisses his cheek. "You know you secretly like the name!"

"Widget is not a name, so there's nothing for me to secretly like!" Shane walked back to his booth, settling down with a stack of paperwork to keep himself occupied.

Kelsi took their order and ran toward the kitchen to show off her poster.

Michelle looked at Steven for a moment. "Why did you go to Jaclyn's house yesterday?"

Steven squirmed a little under her withering look. "Well, she asked me to go. It's a good thing I did, too, because she needed some help changing a light bulb."

"She told me. I asked you to avoid her."

He shrugged. "I had to hear the message the fairies had for me. I've never received a message from fairies before, and it's an exciting thing for me."

She sighed. "I don't think we need any help from the fairies. Do you?"

"Maybe. I can't turn it down, though, because it might offend them. No one wants to be around offended fairies."

"Or any other kind, either!" Michelle shook her head at him. "You don't believe in chiropractors, but you believe in fairies? Do you see the problem with that?"

He shrugged. "I think fairies are beautiful. Can you deny liking Tinkerbell?"

"I don't know much about Tinkerbell other than her appearance in Hook, which I greatly enjoyed. I happen to be a Julia Roberts fan, though."

"I am, too. Loved that movie. It was a fascinating take on the Peter Pan story."

"Are you trying to distract me from the fact that I asked you to do something, and you did the exact opposite? Do you really think that's a good way to start a relationship?"

Steven grinned. "So you think we're in a relationship, do you?"

Michelle sputtered for a moment. "I don't know what else to call it. We're seeing each other every day, and you can't seem to keep your lips to yourself."

Kelsi stopped beside the table. "I'm not sure this is a discussion I'm supposed to hear, so I'm just going to leave your root beers and your cheese curds and slip away quietly."

Michelle felt the heat filling her cheeks. Had she really just been overheard saying that? Normally her private life was kept far from the ranch. "What are you doing to me?" she asked.

Steven shrugged. "I like the cool composed doctor who always knows the right thing to say, but I have to admit this Michelle is very intriguing." He liked the blush that filled her cheeks. Of course, from what he could tell he liked everything about her.

She shook her head, grabbing a cheese curd and popping it in her mouth to keep from saying what she really wanted to say. It wouldn't be appropriate for anyone to overhear, though, so she would stay quiet. "You're starting to get on my nerves, Steven Pickman."

He grinned. "I'm glad. I like knowing I can get under your skin."

Kelsi hurried back with two salads. "I'm not listening to anything you say. I swear I'm not!" And she rushed away from them, causing them both to laugh.

"I love that woman!" Michelle said with a grin.

"She's something else." He wanted to tell her about the demands Kelsi had made for them to be able to film their show there, but he wasn't at liberty to talk about it yet. Not even to Michelle.

"Now about Jaclyn..."

"I'm going to go see her again this afternoon. She reminds me of my grandmother, and I have this need to take care of her. I'll help her out with anything she needs."

Michelle blinked a few times before nodding. "I can't argue with that."

"Good. Then let's stop arguing and eat some of Bob's amazing food."

"You know, you're a pretty darn good cook yourself."

He shrugged. "I enjoy tinkering in the kitchen."

"Do you want to go to the restaurant for trivia tonight? We could get there on time and actually participate."

He nodded. "I hope there's lots of movie trivia, because that's my specialty."

"I do really good with muscles and bones."

"I can see that. You seem like you might be a history buff as well, but I'm not sure."

She nodded with a grin. "Definitely a history buff. And a literature fan. I love literature."

"I can see that. You seem like you'd be someone who'd take a vacation with her nose buried in a book."

"At least it's never stuck in anyone else's business. Being stuck in books is a good thing and good for me."

Steven shrugged, not able to argue. Besides, their stew was there, and he was happy to have more of Bob's cooking to shovel into his face.

Chapter Six

Steven spent most of the afternoon making phone calls, trying to get the cast of *Lazy Love* to agree to make an appearance on the ranch. All of them were busy, and he hated to even ask it of them, but they all knew what this project meant to him.

Finally, he got the agreement of everyone necessary. It was only the main four characters anyone wanted to meet, and they were very loyal to him, making things easy. He thanked them all and helped them with the travel arrangements.

Instead of waiting until the next day, he walked back over to the main house. Once again, he had to speak to Wade's assistant first. She seemed very loyal to him, which told him a lot about the kind of man Wade was. People weren't loyal to bosses who weren't good to them in the first place.

"Sorry to come by unannounced. I know he'll see me, though." Steven hoped he was right. There was the off chance Wade was too busy for him.

The woman nodded. "I've just finished typing up your contract." She pushed a button. "Wade, Steven Pickman is back again."

"Send him in."

Wade was on his feet when Steven opened the door. "Do you have good news for me?"

"Of course, I do. How's this weekend?"

Wade's eyes widened. "This weekend? I figured we'd be booking them in six months or something."

"After I mentioned where I was and how amazing the ranch is, they were all on board. One of the actors met his wife right after she had a writing retreat here on the ranch with Kaya." Steven hadn't connected it was the same ranch until the phone call with Bob.

"Yes, of course! I forgot about that. So she'll be coming, too?"

"Bob said she wouldn't miss seeing Kaya for anything." Steven sat down in the chair across from Wade's desk. "I hear you have a contract for me." He was ready to sign it, unless they were asking for a ridiculous amount of money.

"I do. It's got what we want to be paid, and all of our stipulations for this." Wade pulled a sheaf of papers from a drawer and pushed them across his desk.

Steven looked through them, quickly scanning for the information he needed and making sure he read all the fine print. There was nothing he wanted or needed to change, so he quickly scrawled his signature on the final page. "Can you accommodate three couples, with one child each, on Saturday night? They fly in Saturday afternoon and out on Sunday afternoon. And they're willing to hold an event on Saturday night where people can meet them, and they will sign autographs. I was told this is your quietest time of year, so I didn't think it would be too terribly difficult."

Wade nodded. "I don't think we have an event in the event barn this weekend. It's so close after Christmas that the ranch is pretty quiet. I can clear three cabins as well."

"Sounds good. Thank you!" Steven got to his feet, shaking Wade's hand. "I'm excited that we're going to be able to get going on this project." And now he felt like he could finally talk to Michelle about it. He'd hated hiding his real purpose at the ranch from her.

"I'm excited to see where this goes. I don't think we'd want a lot of crews on the property, but one film crew sounds good to me." Wade seemed as pleased with their agreement as Steven was.

"Is there someone I should talk to about the facilities for the meet and greet?" Steven asked. "I'd like to have all that set up before they get here. And Saturday is just two days away."

"I still can't believe you talked them into coming so quickly." Wade shook his head at him.

"Neither can I, but I'm certainly not complaining." Steven took the name of the person in charge of the event barn and promised to call her immediately. Wade said she was out of the office that afternoon, or Steven could have spoken to her right there.

As he left the main house, he dialed the number he'd been given.

"This is Lily."

"Lily, this is Steven Pickman. I was given your number by Wade. I need to set up an event for Saturday night. He said the event barn would be the best location. Do you know if it's available?"

"It is. What type of event is it?" Lily asked.

"It's going to be a small meet and greet with the actors from the show *Lazy Love*. The four primary actors are coming, and they will be signing posters and meeting fans." Steven had done this type of event with the four of them many times before, so he wasn't worried about how his people would adapt to whatever they gave him to work with. They were all professionals.

"Does Kelsi have something to do with this? She loves that show!"

Steven laughed. "As a matter of fact, she does. I'm one of the directors for the show, so I'm setting it up for her."

"Sounds good to me. Are we opening this to the public?"

He frowned, wondering how much he should push this. "Let's. I don't imagine we'll get too many people with a two-day notice in rural Idaho."

"You might be surprised. I'll get some flyers posted around town, and we'll make sure the guests and staff of the ranch know about it. Refreshments?"

"Yeah, refreshments would be good. What would you normally serve for something like this?" He usually left that type of detail up to whomever was setting up the event.

She made a soft humming sound. "Why don't we do cookies? Finger sandwiches? Does that work for you? I can have punch, coffee, tea, and water to drink."

"That all sounds good. What time?"

"You tell me. You're the one wanting to do the event!"

"Why don't we say from six to nine? My people will be flying in at three Saturday afternoon, so that will give them a little time to settle in and rest before they need to be there."

"Remember we do have a childcare facility on property."

"I will let the actors know. Thank you so much for your help." He paused for a moment, and then added, "Let me give you my phone number so you can let me know if there are any problems or ask me any questions that might come up."

"I have it on my caller ID. I will verify everything with you two hours before the event, and I'll be in touch if there are problems between now and then. Thank you so much for contacting me."

"Thank you!" Steven stuck his phone into his pocket and wondered if Kelsi realized all the hoops she was making people jump through just so she could meet the stars of her favorite show. Even as he thought it, he grinned. He knew Valerie, Amber, and May would all get a huge kick out of Kelsi.

He wandered back toward his cabin, needing to rest for a bit before trivia that evening. He couldn't wait to see Michelle in her element. She seemed as though she loved games to him.

MICHELLE COULDN'T BELIEVE how nervous she was to meet Steven for trivia that night. They'd played trivia together, and spent a whole lot of time together that week, and she was only now getting this nervous? She knew it had something to do with him talking to Jaclyn.

No romance on the ranch was official unless Jaclyn was involved, and now that she was, it kind of freaked her out a little.

She met him in front of the restaurant, waiting as patiently as she did anything else, which is to say, not very patiently at all. "I'm not sure this is a good idea."

Steven looked at her with surprise. "It's not?"

She shook her head. "Everything was fine and even seemed casual until you talked to Jaclyn. That changed everything in my mind—and in everyone else's!" She wasn't sure how to explained just how strong Jaclyn's reputation was as the ranch's matchmaker.

"Why?" She was making no sense to him.

"Because Jaclyn is the ranch matchmaker. No one is official until she's spoken to, and she's been spoken to!" She knew she wasn't making a lot of sense, but she didn't know how to get it across.

He studied her for a moment, trying to understand. "So it was okay to go out with me as long as Jaclyn wasn't involved?"

"Yes! Don't you see? Everything is different now!"

"I really don't see, but I'll take your word for it."

She took a deep breath. "I'm being silly, and I know it, but it's still how I feel. It's as if some imaginary switch was flipped, and now that she knows about us, there's more to it than there was."

Steven frowned. "Would that be such a bad thing? I can't deny I have feelings for you. Do you not have feelings for me?" He hoped he wasn't the only one with feelings, because his were so strong, he couldn't imagine life without her.

"Well, sure I do, but it's just—" He cut her off by grabbing her by the waist and kissing her.

Michelle wound her arms around his neck and clung to him. She wanted everything to be the same...but she also wanted everything to be more. Confusion was not her friend.

When he finally lifted his head, he looked deeply into her eyes. "I think tonight should be a night alone together. No trivia. I have something to tell you, and it should be said in private, I think."

Her heart seemed to skip a beat at his words. She nodded. "All right. Where do you want to go?" Was he going to tell her that he was married with three kids, two dogs, a cat, four birds, and a pet goldfish? Or even a whole *tank* of goldfish?

He shrugged. "Well, we still need to eat, so could we drive into Riston? Seems like there were food options there." He'd only driven to the grocery store in town, so he hadn't paid a lot of attention to restaurants, but surely there was something.

"Sure." She followed him to his cabin and climbed into the passenger seat of his car. "Nice car. Rental?"

"Not really. It belongs to the ranch, and they're letting me use it during my visit."

Michelle frowned at that. "I've never heard of the family just letting someone use a car. That's strange."

"I'm a unique case, and I'm going to explain all about why when we sit down for supper. What's the quietest restaurant in Riston?" He didn't want any distractions when he told her about his real purpose there.

"Um...most of the restaurants are more family dining than anything else. Why don't we pick something up and take it to my place?"

"Perfect. Where should we pick something up from?"

"There's a small pizza place, and the pizza is really good. You'd think it was a more expensive restaurant, it's so good."

"Tell me how to get there," Steven said.

While he drove, she phoned in an order so they wouldn't have to wait as long. She strained her brain, trying to remember if she'd managed to make her bed that morning. She tried to do it every day, but sometimes it just didn't happen.

The pizza was waiting for them when they got there, and they took it straight back to her place. She had half of a duplex, and he parked in the driveway, very interested in where she lived.

"I'll get the pizza. You get the door."

Michelle hurried to the door, unlocking and opening it, then she flipped on a light and looked around, making sure it was neat before she let him in.

She smiled to herself. She'd even put her breakfast dishes into the dishwasher and made her bed. Nothing to complain about there.

He walked in behind her, looking around. There were mementos of her travels everywhere. She had told him she'd spent three years working in Australia, and there were some Aboriginal art pieces on the walls. "Very nice."

She smiled, thankful that her panic over the state of her house had been for nothing. It truly didn't look bad at all. She got down plates and glasses, getting them each a glass of ice water, and then they served their pizza and took it to the table to eat it.

"I can't believe how good this pizza tastes. I don't think I realized quite how hungry I was."

Steven took a bite and nodded. "This really is good. They need to franchise."

"Nah. Then it wouldn't be our special little secret anymore." Michelle loved having special things in Riston, Idaho that no one else in the world had.

He smiled at that. "So...I came to the ranch to check it out and try to make a deal with the Westons. Have you read Kaya's book about the Westons' ancestors?"

Michelle nodded. "Sure. I think everyone on the ranch has. It was a good marketing ploy for her, because we all wanted autographed copies. Why?"

"Well, someone sent it to me and told me it should be a television series, and I read it. I loved it, and I decided to head up the project as an executive producer, which is a new role for me. It's always been something I knew I would eventually do, but it wasn't the right time—until now."

"Why didn't you just tell me that when we met?"

"I said I'd keep it quiet until we had a location for filming. I should have told you, but I just didn't feel like I could and keep my word to my partners on the project." He reached out and took her hand in his. "Forgive me?"

"There's really nothing to forgive. You weren't obligated to tell me anything." Michelle was surprised to find she felt a little hurt by his lack of honesty with her though. Not that he'd lied...he just wasn't forthcoming with all the details.

"No, I wasn't obligated, but for our relationship to go anywhere, I do need to tell you everything from here on out. I signed a contract with Wade today. One of the stipulations was that I get the four main stars from *Lazy Love* here to sign autographs."

Michelle couldn't help but be amused by that. "Kelsi?"

"Who else? So I spent half the afternoon on the phone getting the four of them to agree, and then the other half was spent with Wade signing the contract and on the phone with Lily setting up the event. It'll be on Saturday night in the event barn. I was hoping you'd go as my date." He knew it was a stretch for her, and would be completely out of her comfort zone, but it was important to him.

"What kind of event are we talking about? Am I expected to wear a dress? Can I wear slacks?"

He shrugged. "It's going to be the four actors signing posters. I'll have to wear a suit, because I'm a director and I'm putting the whole thing together to amuse Kelsi. Lily is going to have some cookies and stuff out. Punch, tea, coffee, and water. That kind of thing."

"So it would definitely mean a dress." She had nothing else happening, and she would love to meet his co-workers. But...why was she so nervous about the whole thing? And why did she feel betrayed by him? "How is using the ranch to shoot a television show going to change things?"

"A commissary will be built for the cast and staff. There will also be a big parking lot built across the highway for the actors' trailers. A building will be built for the inside scenes but all outdoor scenes will be filmed in the Old West town. We'll be allowed to shoot in the Old West town only on Tuesdays and Thursdays, and all of the guests will be considered to be extras if they choose to be. It's all been worked out so we'll have the least impact on the day-to-day business of the ranch."

"That's probably good." She took another bite of her pizza, watching him. "Why do you want me there?"

He blinked at her. "Because I have feelings for you, and I want you to meet all the people I love. Is that so hard to understand?" He couldn't believe she'd even ask him that.

She sighed. "I guess I have to go, then. I'll figure out something to wear." Her idea of dressing up was wearing a pair of slacks for work. Her dress clothes never included a dress or a skirt. She wasn't fond of either, so she simply didn't wear them. She could see that this was something she'd have to make an exception for.

"I'd like to pick you up at five, if I may?" All of a sudden, Steven felt like he needed to be formal with her. Their usual zing was missing, and he wasn't sure if it was because he'd talked to Jaclyn or because he hadn't told her the real reason he was there. "I can't imagine going without you by my side."

Michelle smiled at that. "Then that's where I'll be." She took a sip of her water. "To tell the truth, I'm looking forward to meeting the four main stars of the show. It'll be interesting to see what they're like in real life."

"Well, Jesse and Valerie—who play Dylan and Jo—are as much in love off-screen as they are on. Valerie was in a horrible relationship for years, and Jesse helped her get out of it. They really do belong together. I remember when we auditioned them for the parts. They were total strangers, but when they kissed at that audition, it was like two souls meant to be together were finding each other. I know that sounds sappy, but I think every single person in that studio felt that way."

She grinned at him. "Who would have thought you'd be such a softie!"

He shrugged. "I wanted my stars happy, and trust me, I've never met a happier couple. It's like they were destined to be together, and both of them knew it the second they met."

"I think that's lovely! Hearing all that makes me really want to meet them. Am I right in thinking they have a child, too?"

"Yes. His name is Jaron, and he's almost a year old. Sweet little boy. They'll bring him as well. I'm not sure how they'll handle that for the signing, but they'll have a plan. They *always* have a plan."

"We have a twenty-four seven child care here on the ranch. The Kids' Korral. Miranda's mother runs it, and it's amazing. All of the Westons leave their kids there, so you know it's good."

"I'll let them know!" He glanced at the time on his phone. "You know what? I need to call them now if you don't mind. There's a time difference, and I don't want to risk waking the baby, who goes to bed ridiculously early."

"Yeah, sure." She sat alone with her pizza while he walked off and made the call. Her mind wouldn't leave her alone, telling her he was only telling her now because she was sure to find out anyway. It was a sad feeling to have. She wanted him to be upfront with her about everything all the time. Relationships needed to have complete honesty, in her opinion. She had to wonder if he was even capable of it.

There was certainly a huge difference between the lifestyle he was used to in California and the slow-paced life of Idaho. She was certain people here were more honest, and that's what she was used to.

Chapter Seven

Steven left Michelle's house that night, a bit worried that she was upset with him over the whole thing. He knew she hadn't wanted him to talk to Jaclyn, and he sort of understood, but he was still pleased that he had. It wasn't like they were married and she had the right to control his every move. She wouldn't even if they were married.

He sighed. He was just making excuses. He'd done something knowing it would displease her, and that hadn't been right. Hiding his true purpose at the ranch from her hadn't been good, either. He'd just have to make sure that he was better to her from now on, so she would see...see what? What did he want her to see? That he was the only man in the world for her?

Maybe. Maybe his problem was that she was annoyed, and he was already falling in love with her. How was he supposed to deal with that?

He pulled up in front of the cabin where he was staying to find Jaclyn lurking with a different bunny on a leash.

"Sometimes you make me feel like I'm under surveillance."

She laughed heartily. "I promise I'm not with the FBI. I'm just a regular, old-fashioned woman who talks to fairies on a regular basis."

"Well, ask the fairies why she's upset with me, would you? Or better yet—because I'm pretty sure I know why—ask them how to get her to stop being upset with me." If he was frustrated enough to ask questions of the local fairy-whisperer, he was even further gone than he realized.

Jaclyn walked to him and patted his arm. "She'll get over it. She knows you're the man for her, and it's just hard for her to come to grips with that. She's thirty-three years old and has always had her freedom. You're the man who can take it away from her, and she's scared. She's looking for reasons to break it off with you. Don't let her."

"But if she'd be happier without me, then shouldn't I just let her go?"

Jaclyn shook her head. "Trust me when I say she would *not* be better off without you. I liked my freedom, and I spent too long asking the man I loved to wait just a little longer. The day I decided to accept his offer to marry me, he was killed in the line of duty. He was a police officer, you see." Jaclyn shrugged. "I'm always surrounded by people I love. The fairies will never let me be lonely. When you meet that special someone you're meant to spend forever with, you can't give it up. Neither of you will be happier." She sighed. "I know I'll never be able to replace him in my heart."

Steven frowned at her. He hadn't expected something so touching to be said by a woman walking a bunny. "I'll think about what you said." Like he'd be able to think about anything else.

"Good. I don't want you to make a mistake that will ruin two lives simply because you're stubborn."

"I'm not stubborn!" What was she talking about?

Jaclyn just patted his arm and walked away toward her house.

He frowned after her, shaking his head. The woman must have been put on this earth simply to drive him batty. There was no other explanation at all.

WHEN STEVEN WENT TO his appointment the next day, Michelle was even a bit more withdrawn than she'd been. "I'm sorry," he said, not quite sure exactly what he was wrong about, but he was pretty sure that's what she needed to hear from him.

"You are?" Michelle asked, narrowing her eyes. "What exactly are you sorry for?"

"Umm..."

She sighed. "I'm not really angry with you. I'm just a bit confused about what I need to do next." She almost said she'd never been in love before, but he didn't need that little piece of information quite yet.

"Next, go to the party with me tomorrow night and have fun. What's so hard about that?"

"Nothing I guess. I just feel like you might not have the ability to be as honest as I need you to be. We're from very different worlds..."

"Maybe we are, but that doesn't mean we can't meet in the middle. And I wasn't born and raised in California." He caught her chin and met her eyes. "I'm willing to make the compromises that need to be made for the two of us to work things out. Getting to know each other a little better is the best first step, of course. And I badly want you to meet some of the people I care about this weekend. All right?"

Michelle nodded, feeling a bit sad and lost. She'd always been a confident woman who spent a lot of time training to be a strong business leader. Never had she expected a man to come along and knock her on her butt. "I'll do my best."

"Good girl."

"Lunch?" he asked as soon as his appointment was over.

She nodded, but she did so less eagerly than before. He was worried that he'd ruined things completely, but he certainly hoped not.

On their walk to the café, she walked a couple feet away from him, instead of right beside him as she had before. "Just so you know, not everyone knows about the filming taking place on the ranch. I believe it's only the Weston family, and you, of course. Because you're very important to me."

She looked at him for a moment. "Are you sure I'm not just some vacation romance who you'll forget as soon as you go back to work?"

"If I thought that was even a possibility, I wouldn't have tried to start anything with you. If I went back to work tomorrow, I'd never be able to get your big green eyes out of my mind. You're very special to me, Michelle, and I aim to prove it."

"I wish you could! Proving it very quickly would alleviate my mind a lot. I'm usually one of the most confident women around. I don't know what you're doing to me!"

"Whatever it is, I promise you it's unintentional."

As soon as they were seated, Kelsi hurried over with the menus. "I can't believe they're really going to be here tomorrow! How did you do it?"

Steven grinned at her, having no problem following her train of thought. "They're my friends, and they know it will help me with my new project. What's so strange about that?"

"Whatever the reason, I couldn't be more excited! I didn't sleep a wink last night, and for once, that wasn't because of two babies wanting to be held at the same time." Kelsi glanced over as new people came in. "Special today is cheese enchiladas. They're not as good as mine, but they're not bad considering they were made by a Bob."

Steven had learned his lesson. "That's what I'm having."

"Me too." Michelle pushed her menu away. "I want root beer today, too." It was a root beer kind of day. She wasn't a drinker, but she was always willing to drown her sorrows in a huge vat of root beer.

"Me too," he said. He reached out and took Michelle's hand in his as Kelsi walked away. "I'm sorry that I'm making your day rough. I only want what's best for you."

"And you think you're what's best for me?"

He shrugged. "I think I could be if you'd let me. Don't shut me out because I couldn't tell you something. If you had a patient come see you and they told you something confidential, would you tell me?"

"Well, no I couldn't, but..."

"Yeah...see, that's how I felt. It was something I promised my partners I'd keep quiet until we had a signed contract. We have one now."

She sighed. "I guess that makes sense. It just feels so strange that you couldn't tell me the truth right away. It almost hurt when I found out that you hadn't been upfront. That and the whole Jaclyn thing..."

"The Jaclyn thing is something I still don't feel like I did wrong on. I know you didn't want me to talk to her, but I half thought you were kidding. And she reminds me so much of my grandmother, I couldn't stay away. I'd do that again tomorrow."

She frowned. "I guess that makes sense. I don't really have the right to ask you not to talk to people...I just felt uncomfortable with it."

He looked into her eyes. "Can we get past this?"

"Yeah. We can get past it."

"So I'll see you this evening."

"Nope. I have to figure out what I'm wearing to your big thing tomorrow night."

He grinned. "Because you're going as my date to meet my friends and declare to the whole world that the fairies are with us?"

"Don't get sucked into the fairy madness!" Michelle couldn't help but grin. The whole ranch was nuts over fairies, and she didn't need him to be part of that...but it was cute that he was thinking about it.

"But it's so fun! I can't wait to introduce Bob to Jaclyn. She's going to freak him out majorly."

Michelle laughed, shaking her head. "Is he super uptight?"

"I wouldn't say uptight...he just doesn't like a lot of weird stuff. May has changed him a lot, though."

"In what way?"

Steven shook his head. "It's hard to put my finger on, but he's more laid back. Easier to joke with. His whole face lights up whenever he looks at her. Kind of amazes me sometimes."

"That's really cool. I can't wait to meet both of them." Michelle found she really was looking forward to meeting them—not because they were stars of the television show she was starting to like, but because they were his friends and they would have some insight into him.

After lunch, they went their separate ways, and he called Lily to make sure everything was coming along well. After that call was managed, he made his way over to see Jaclyn. Instead of talking to her about the fairies, he shoveled her front walk, assuring her that he was fine to do so.

"I'm not in pain, so I can handle it with no problem. Dr. Michelle just wants to keep seeing me because she's smitten."

Jaclyn laughed from her vantage point on the steps, where she had three bunnies hopping around her and another on her lap. "Smitten? Is that word even used anymore? Mind you, I like it, but that's because I'm as old as dirt."

He put the shovel in the snow and leaned on it, looking at her. "Still look beautiful to me, Jaclyn!"

"Don't be wasting your sweet words on me! My heart was buried long before you were born!"

"Waste of a beautiful woman."

"Does that mean you're going to let me be an extra on the television show of yours?" she asked.

He couldn't help but grin at that. "Do you want to be?"

"Why not? I've got some moments of craziness left in me."

"I can see that. No doubt in my mind."

"When you're done with that, will you take out my trash and help me with the litter box?" she asked.

He grinned. "Are you trying to take advantage of my helpfulness?"

"Of course I am. I may be old, but I'm not stupid!"

When he was finished with all the chores Jaclyn had for him, Steven walked toward the Old West town. There was something about the place that drew him, and he couldn't seem to stay away.

He went into the bakery and bought a cookie and a bottle of water from Miranda. "Are you baking for the big party tomorrow night?" he asked.

She nodded. "I'm going to be there, too. Love the show."

"I'm glad. I'll introduce you to the stars if you'd like."

"Will they be mingling with us lesser people, or just sitting behind tables to sign stuff?" Miranda asked.

"I'll make sure they do a little of both."

"Oh, good. I can't wait!"

He paid and left the little bakery, walking toward the infirmary to thank Bridget for her help. When he got there, he found her in the back alone. "Just came to say thank you for your help."

Bridget grinned at him. "Looks like Dr. Michelle fixed you up pretty well."

He nodded. "She did. She's pretty fabulous, even if she is a quack."

Bridget laughed. "Don't tell her she's a quack. Then she'll let your back rot off you."

The door opened behind him and a tall blonde walked in. "Midget! Did you hear? My friend May is going to be here tomorrow! Along with her Bob, who I haven't even met yet!"

Steven studied the newcomer for a moment. "Are you Kaya?"

She nodded. "I am. Who are you?"

He held his hand out. "We've spoken on the phone. I'm Steven Pickman."

Kaya looked at him for a moment before a smile spread across her face. "You're making my book into a television series!"

He nodded. "That's why I'm at the ranch. I've signed a contract with Wade Weston to film the pilot here starting next month."

"Then you're the one bringing May and the others here, right?"

"It was a stipulation of the contract."

Kaya threw back her head and laughed. "Kelsi."

"Yes. She certainly knows what she wants, and meeting all the stars of the show is all she wants out of life, apparently. So I'm bringing them here so she can meet them."

"I think that's awesome." Kaya looked at Bridget. "And you know my sister?"

"Yeah, she helped me after I fell off the mountain." Steven blinked a couple of times. "Didn't I hear you two are twins? There are no two people who look less like twins..."

Kaya grinned at that. "Ignore the hair and the height and just look at our faces."

His eyes widened. "I do see it! You look a lot alike. It's just unnerving how much taller you are."

"I'm more than a foot taller than Midget here, but I am older by a whole five minutes."

"I'm glad to finally meet you. We'll need to sit down for a bit while I'm here and talk about some specifics. I have some changes in mind for the show, and I want to talk about the stars I want to bring in for it."

"Sounds good. When do you leave?"

"Monday. Could we meet up Monday morning? I should have contacted you before, but I've been a bit distracted since I got here."

"He *fell off the mountain*," Bridget interjected. "And from the rumors I'm hearing, he's got something going with Dr. Michelle."

Steven felt the heat rise into his face. Blushing? He was thirty-four years old and had been working in the film industry for ten years. He couldn't blush in front of people. "I refuse to answer that."

Kaya grinned. "I'll ask her myself. I have an appointment in a few minutes." She headed toward the door. "Bridget, you have to go tomorrow night. And no Cinderella talk. People already think you're nuts."

"Go away, Kaya!" Bridget called after her sister.

"Cinderella talk?" Steven asked after Kaya was gone.

"Oh, I like to ask people who their favorite Disney princess is, because mine's Cinderella, but I haven't even done that for a couple of days. Kaya likes to think of me how I *used to* be."

He laughed at that. "You two gave your mother a run for her money, didn't you?"

"Mom always says there's a reason she never had any more."

"I can see that." He headed toward the door. "I want to go and check out the saloon, and then I have a few more phone calls to make. I need to make sure my people are settled happily before the event tomorrow."

"See ya!" Bridget waved to him and went back to playing Yahtzee on her phone. She was addicted, and she wasn't even ashamed of it.

Steven walked toward the saloon, having heard wonderful things about the coffee Sadie offered there. He opened the door and went in, sitting on a barstool. "I want to pound my fist on the counter and ask for a sarsaparilla, but I think I'll just have a caramel latte instead."

A woman walked toward him with a smile. "I'll get it for you right away! You want that for here or to go?"

"Oh, to go, I think. I've been having fun wandering around the ranch."

"It's a beautiful place, isn't it?" She pulled some levers on a machine in front of her. "Have you heard the cast of *Lazy Love* is signing autographs tomorrow night? I'm pretty excited, I have to admit."

"I'm one of the directors of the show, and I arranged for them to be here. I'm Steven Pickman."

"Oh, that's exciting! Why are you having them all come? That's the one thing I didn't understand."

"I needed something from the ranch, and to get the Westons to sign a contract, I had to agree to bring them here."

"Kelsi?" Sadie asked.

"Does everyone know about her obsession with the show? You're like the fourth person who's automatically asked if it was Kelsi."

"Yeah...Kelsi doesn't hide a whole lot. I'm seriously still trying to figure out how she hid the fact she was having twins until she went into labor. Big surprise from someone like Kelsi."

"I like her. She's waited on my table several times."

"Enjoying Bob's cooking?" she asked.

"More than I could ever express. I'm ready to pack up and move to Idaho just so I can eat at the diner every day."

She laughed, handing him his drink. "Well, I'm not sure that's the answer, but I wouldn't blame you. I'll see you at the party tomorrow."

"I'll be there!"

Chapter Eight

Kaya rushed into the chiropractic office as Michelle was finishing up notes on her previous patient.

"Hi. How're you feeling today? Anything new?"

Instead of answering, Kaya hurried to her and hugged her. "*Lazy Love* is coming to the ranch!"

Michelle laughed. "I know that."

"I know you know. Bridget says you're dating Steven, and he's producing my book. Or he's producing the TV series based on my book. Yeah, that makes more sense."

Michelle shrugged. "I don't know if dating is the right word for it. We're seeing each other a lot, though."

"Tell me about it!"

"Let's get you adjusted, and then we'll talk. I might even beg you to go shopping with me this evening. I need a dress to wear to that thing, because I'm going as his date, and he's wearing a suit, and I don't *wear* dresses."

"I would love to go shopping with you. Who's a better person to shop with a tall, lanky woman than another tall, lanky woman? We'll find you something in green to match your eyes. I can't wait to see you look beautiful!"

Michelle grinned. "Are you saying I'm not already beautiful?"

"I'm a writer. I refuse to let you use my own tools against me." Kaya smiled at her friend. "When do you close?"

"You're my last patient."

"Then I'm going to call Glen, and we're going to Lewiston. There's got to be a gorgeous dress with your name on it there!"

Michelle fought with herself for a moment. Money wasn't the issue. She just didn't want to have to "change" for a man. But wearing a dress one night wasn't really changing for him was it? She sighed heavily. "Yeah, call Glen. We'll take my car, and we'll find some amazing food to eat while we're gone, because I need amazing food."

They left minutes later, taking Michelle's car. It wasn't meant for the Idaho roads in winter, but she didn't care at the moment. They hadn't had a snowfall in a couple of days, and the roads should be clear.

While they drove, Kaya peppered her with questions about Steven, and Michelle did her best not to answer them. "Why don't you ask *him* all this?" Michelle finally asked. "I haven't known him very long."

"You love him, don't you?" Kaya asked, her voice softer and more serious than it had been all day.

Michelle shrugged. "What does it matter if I do? He's here for a vacation, and he's going home on Monday."

"Maybe he is...maybe he isn't. And who says you can't go with him when he leaves? I came here on vacation, and came back a couple of weeks later as Glen's wife. This place has made more romances than I can count...and all of them seem to be happy marriages. There's something special about the ranch. The Westons should have called it Romance Ranch, not River's End."

Michelle smiled. "Maybe. I just don't know what to do at the moment, so I'm trying not to let my heart get too involved—"

"Too late."

"Yeah, it probably *is* too late. But...I want to be happy, and rein myself in just a little. I worry that he's going to leave and take my heart with him. And what good would I be if I were heartless?"

"True." Kaya stared at the road in front of her. "But I think you need to give him a chance. Let your heart be open to him. There's no point in closing yourself off."

"I'm not. I'm shopping for a dress, aren't I?" Michelle didn't know what else she was supposed to do. Shopping for a dress for a man seemed like the ultimate sacrifice to her.

Kaya obviously realized she needed to change the subject. "So, what do you want for supper? I'm in the mood for Mexican."

"I'm *always* in the mood for Mexican!"

IT WAS DARK EARLY IN January, and the night seemed to drag. Steven tried watching some old movies, but he couldn't seem to get into any of them. This was the first evening since he'd met Michelle that they hadn't spent together.

Normally he had no problem with his own company, but he really missed her, which seemed odd with as short a time as they'd known one another. How had she already come to fill up his every thought?

He read for a while and went to bed early, Michelle's face on the back of his eyelids.

MICHELLE MET STEVEN at the café the following day for lunch. Her office was closed for the weekend, and she was too nervous about the event that night to think about patients anyway. It was strange how uncomfortable a formal event made her feel.

When he saw her walking toward him, he hurried toward her, pulling her to him and kissing her softly. "Last night felt like an eternity. I can't believe how used to having you around I've become."

"Really? Went by fast for me." She loved teasing him. For some reason his admission made her feel like they were on more even footing.

"Did you find what you were looking for?"

She shrugged. "I think so. I hope you're all right if I don't look like a movie star. I will do my best to look like a dressed-up chiropractor."

"Works for me. I can't wait to introduce you to my friends. They should be getting to the ranch in about two hours. Frank is picking them up in Lewiston."

"Am I meeting you at the event barn?" she asked, hoping she was. Then she could slip out early if she was too uncomfortable. She was an introvert through and through, and the evening was downright frightening to her.

"Would you be willing to meet me at my cabin instead? I'd like you to meet my friends before the event."

"But that means I have to wear a dress longer!"

He laughed. "You can handle it. I promise!"

She groaned but nodded. "I'll be there. What time?"

"Four?"

She felt a moment of panic at his words. They wouldn't be finished eating until one or two, and she had a lot to do to get ready. She wasn't used to being all girly. "I can do that."

"I promise, you're going to like them, and it'll be worth every minute of your time."

"I hope so."

Kelsi was floating around the café, obviously excited about the evening. "I'm putting the twins in the Kids' Korral. I haven't had a Saturday out in a million years, and I'm going to enjoy every single second of it."

Michelle grinned. "I'm glad you're so excited. Are there going to be photo opportunities?"

Kelsi looked at Steven. "I didn't even think of that. What about photo ops, Steven?"

"Sure. I can make that happen." Steven knew he was going to owe his friends big time at the end of the night, but they would be good sports about everything. That's the kind of friends they were.

Kelsi clapped a couple of times. "I'm going to remember this night for the rest of my life!"

After she was gone, Steven took Michelle's hand. "I'm going to remember this night for the rest of my life, too. It'll be the first night I ever see you dressed up."

"And the last," she mumbled under her breath.

He laughed. "I'm not so sure about that. I have lots of award shows and stuff I'm required to attend."

"Yes, but you're a director-producer person. I'm just a chiropractor. I fix broken people."

"But you'll come with me if I beg, won't you?" He couldn't imagine not having his wife attend things with him. As soon as the words flitted through his mind, he knew that she needed to be his bride. But he couldn't imagine that she'd agree on such a short acquaintance. He had to try, though. For both of their sakes.

MICHELLE SPENT THE afternoon getting ready for her evening with Steven. She didn't care what his friends thought of her. She just wanted to not embarrass him. After showering and fixing her long auburn hair, she dressed in the forest green, slim-skirted gown that she and Kaya had chosen for her.

She looked at herself in the mirror and almost took it off again. How could she have thought she could pull this off? She felt like a little girl playing dress-up in her mother's closet. She'd not gone to prom or any other big dance at school. Dressing up wasn't something she'd ever enjoyed or wanted to do, so she simply hadn't bothered.

Closing her eyes, she forced her breathing to calm. She could make it through this. Who would have thought someone as confident as she was would have a panic attack at the idea of being around strangers all night while wearing a dress? What was wrong with her?

She fixed her make-up carefully, putting some into her purse for a touch-up should she need it as the night wore on.

Slipping her feet into comfortable flats, she walked out to the car through the falling snow. She wanted to curse the snow, but what good would that do? At least everyone would have had to go through snow the same as her to get to the party.

When she arrived at Steven's cabin at just before four, she sat in her car for a moment, staring at the house. Surely no one wanted her to be there early. She should turn around and go back home and show up for the party like a normal person.

Just as she decided she should do just that, Steven stepped outside, looking sexy as anything she'd ever seen. He wore a black tuxedo and a black tie. She stared at him, swallowing hard. Was he really her date for the night?

He walked to her car and opened the door for her. "You were about to go home, weren't you?"

She shrugged. "I would have gone to the party. I promise."

"Well, you're coming inside to meet my friends. I made supper." She got out of the car and nodded, feeling totally out of place, and then she looked at his face and saw the appreciation in his eyes. "Do you have any idea how very beautiful you look this evening?"

"I feel like I'm a little girl playing dress-up in her mother's closet, but I never did that. I was too busy playing football outside with the boys. Or practicing gymnastics. I didn't have time for that nonsense."

"Well, you certainly don't look like a little girl playing dress-up. You look like the strong, confident, beautiful woman I know you are. Come meet my friends." He offered his arm, and she took it, still feeling very out of place, but thankful that he was beside her as she walked into a house full of people she didn't know.

As soon as she stepped inside, the girl that played Jo—Valerie was her name—came up to her. "You must be Michelle. I've heard wonderful things about you."

Michelle was surprised when Valerie hugged her as if she was an old friend, but she was a hugger, so she happily hugged back. "And you're Valerie. I've been watching the show with Steven." She leaned forward and said in a dramatic stage whisper. "I wasn't a fan until he made me start from the beginning."

Valerie laughed. "I'm so glad he made you start from the beginning, then, because we need you as a fan." She waved a man forward, who was holding a little boy who looked to be right at a year old. "This is my husband Jesse, and our son, Jaron."

Michelle nodded, smiling. "Hi, Jesse." She was much more comfortable with children than she was with adults, so when Jaron leaned toward her, she had no problem holding him. "Hello, Jaron. I'm Michelle."

Jaron simply stuck two fingers in his mouth and sucked on them as he studied her.

Michelle laughed looking at Valerie. "He's beautiful."

"Thank you. I made him myself!"

"He looks just like his father, which isn't fair. He didn't go through the pain of having him!"

Valerie shrugged. "It's a good thing I love my husband and think he's terribly handsome, isn't it?"

"It is." Michelle felt her gaze going to Steven as she wondered what their children would look like.

Valerie moved closer, dropping her voice so no one could hear. "You love him. It's plain on your face. He's a good man."

"Glad to hear it. It seems like it, but I've only known him since Monday. That's not long enough to be sure of anything."

"Trust me." Valerie took Jaron and stepped back. He put his head on her shoulder happily. "You need to come meet May and Amber. You're going to love them. They're the sisters of my heart. I have a sister, but I don't get to see her as often as I like."

Valerie led Michelle across the room to two women who were sitting together. One was a bit overweight, and obviously not from the show. She was bouncing a little girl on her knee. "May, this is Michelle, Steven's girl. Michelle, this is May, otherwise known as Jolene Gold."

Michelle frowned. "Jolene Gold sounds familiar...wait! I've read some of your books!"

May smiled. "I hope you enjoyed them."

"Enough to look for more of them! It's good to meet you."

"You too. I hear Steven fell off a mountain, and you're the one who fixed him. Very appreciated." May jiggled the baby on her lap. "This is Bobbette, but I call her Bobbi."

"Interesting choice of names!" Michelle wondered how May would respond to that.

"I name so many people in books that I just couldn't name another human being, so I gave Bob carte blanche. It's a different name, but she's a special little girl, and she'll do just fine with it."

Michelle nodded. "I think she will."

Valerie touched Michelle's arm. "This is Amber. She plays MaryBeth on the show." She gestured across the room. "All of our men are over there hanging out, but you don't want to meet them anyway."

"Except Bob," May said very seriously. "Life would never be the same without Bob."

Michelle grinned, nodding toward Amber. "It's nice to meet you."

"Nice to meet you, too. And this is my little girl, Nicki."

Nicki looked at Michelle. "Do you like to play Barbies?"

Michelle sat down so she was eye level with the girl. "I haven't played Barbies in a whole lot of years, but I bet I'd like it just as much as I did when I was a little girl. Did you bring any Barbies with you?"

Nicki nodded solemnly. "I did. But Mama made me leave them in our cabin. Do you want to come to our cabin to play Barbies?"

"I would honestly love to!" Michelle wasn't as uncomfortable as she'd thought she would be, but she still would give just about anything to escape for a few minutes.

Amber shook her head. "It's not a good time to play Barbies. Sorry, Nicki."

Nicki frowned. "But I get to go to the kids' place and not go to the dress-up party, right?"

"Right."

Michelle noticed that Nicki was in jeans and a sweat shirt while all the adult women were dressed in formal dresses. Michelle looked at May. "How do you make it through these things?"

May shrugged. "I swallow my introvert and pretend to be happy where I am. It's not easy."

"Do you do a lot of book signings?"

"As few as I can possibly get away with. I do what's expected of me and very little more. I find that it's easier for me if I do the public appearances with Bob, and I keep my own to an absolute minimum." May sighed. "I wish I could be happy in front of a camera, but I never have been, and I doubt I ever will be."

"I think we have that very much in common. I deal with people all day long when they come into my office, but usually on my lunch break, I go to lunch alone and just sit there and destress. Sometimes I even eat in my office just so I don't have to look at people."

"I understand completely." May grinned at her. "Friends in introversion!"

"Definitely! Kaya and I went shopping last night, and she told me a lot about you. She's very excited you're here."

"I'm excited to see her, too. We've been writing friends for years. We both tend to write through the night and sleep during the day. Thank heavens for nannies!"

Michelle grinned. "Did you bring your nanny?"

May shook her head. "No, I gave her the weekend off. We'll use the childcare here on the ranch for the event, and I'll take care of her the rest of the time."

"That's probably for the best."

"It definitely is. She misses her mommy time when I'm working a lot, like I have been lately. I need to cut down, and I say I will every year, and every year, I don't. I don't know what my problem is."

"Too many stories in your head that have to go onto a computer or you'll lose your mind?"

"That's probably exactly what it is!" May laughed. "You must know Kaya pretty well if you know that's how a writer's mind works."

"She comes to see me every week like clockwork. We're doing what we can to keep her carpal tunnel at bay. I'm amazed at how hard she works."

May nodded. "She's a very hard worker. That's why we're good writing partners."

"I'm glad you two are going to get to see each other tonight. It should be fun for both of you."

Michelle leaned back in her chair, crossing her legs. She watched the others talk and tried to sink back into the background. She liked his friends, and she was glad she got to meet them. Now she wanted to go home and put her Michelle clothes back on.

Chapter Nine

By the time they headed to the party at the event barn, Michelle felt more comfortable with the people around her. Michelle and Steven drove over together, while the other three couples took their children to the Kids' Korral, which had been notified that they would have some extras dropping in that evening.

"How do you like my friends?" he asked as soon as they were alone.

"I really do. They seem very down to earth, even though they're famous."

"Well, John isn't famous, but he's the only one of the six who isn't. Imagine what it would be like for him to run in those circles."

"He seems like a good guy. He's got to feel a bit intimidated, though." Michelle parked the car in the huge parking lot beside the event barn. "May doesn't seem to realize she's famous. Well, none of the ladies really did, but May was as laid back as a person could be."

"Yeah, she's easy to be friends with," he said softly. "Are you ready for this?"

She shrugged. "I feel out of place, which I've said a million times, but I'll make it work. I've never done anything that was this dressy in my life, so I feel a little weird, but whatever."

He leaned toward her planning to kiss her. "You'll be the most beautiful woman there."

"You can't kiss me! You're going to smear my lipstick!"

He frowned. "Don't you have more?"

"I didn't think about that. Yeah, go for it." She caught the back of his head and pulled him to her for a kiss. "I needed that."

He laughed. "I did, too. Let's get in there. Party officially starts in ten minutes, and I'm the host, so I need to get in there and make sure everything is right. And you can go fix your lipstick."

She got out of the car, still feeling silly, but pushing on. At least she knew most of the people in the area. She didn't know why that made it easier, but it did. Side-by-side with Steven, she walked into the building, looking around at the arrangements that had been made. She was always impressed when Lily worked her magic. The event barn had looked like a dozen different places for different events.

She hurried to the bathroom and fixed her lipstick before going back out into the main room to walk back to Steven. She hoped he'd have time for her so she wasn't left standing around looking like a wallflower.

Steven was making sure the spots for his four stars were good. They all had bottles of water at their spots, and they could easily get some of the snack foods that circled the room.

"What do you think?" she asked.

He shrugged. "Looks good. Everything I asked for has been included. I'll make sure the stars are seated before anyone else comes in. We've decided to do an hour of autographs, and hour of mingling, and an hour of pictures with the stars. Hopefully that will make Kelsi happy."

Michelle laughed. "Just being in the room with them will make her happy. Don't let her ask for any of their used napkins as they come into the room, all right?"

Steven shook his head. "They've all heard it before."

"Yeah, but it's still got to be creepy."

"Oh, it is!"

The three couples came in then, Jesse leading the way with Valerie. "How's this going to go?"

Steven nodded to the table. "The four of you will start out behind the table signing autographs for an hour, then mingling for an hour, and then photographs with anyone who wants them for an hour. That work for all of you?"

Jesse nodded, leading Valerie behind the table and sitting down with her. Amber and Bob took their places. "Okay, we're protected by this flimsy table," Jesse said. "I guess we should let them in."

Steven frowned. "I didn't think about security for this event. Are you worried?"

Jesse shook his head. "Just joking. We're going to be fine."

After Valerie's sister's kidnapping almost two years before, Steven had a hard time joking about security. "All right. I'm going to let Lily, the lovely lady who put this event together, know that you're ready."

Michelle wondered what she was supposed to do next, but she drifted over toward May. "I feel completely out of place. You?"

"I'd rather be in a dark room with my fingers on my keyboard. I wouldn't mind coming to these events if I was allowed to just observe and turn people into book characters. Having to actually talk to people like I'm happy to be here is a lot harder for me."

"I think we're going to get along very well. If you need out, let me know—you fake a back injury, and I'll take you to my office for a few minutes."

May laughed. "I hope it won't come to that, but if it does, I'm going to be ready."

"Me, too!" Michelle watched as they opened the main doors to the event barn, and people started swarming inside. Obviously, word had gotten out about the *Lazy Love* stars being there, because this was the biggest crowd she'd ever seen at the barn. Even the weddings she'd been to hadn't been quite as large.

Kelsi was one of the first people to walk up to the table, and watching her reaction warmed Michelle's heart. As soon as she was within five feet of the tables, tears started streaming. "I can't believe you're actually here so I get to meet you. This is amazing!"

Shane put his arm around her and led her to the table. "This is my wife, Kelsi Clapper. She's the one who came up with the ridiculous provision that the four of you needed to come here, because she wanted to meet all of you."

Valerie smiled. "I wondered if it was you." She pulled a headshot of herself toward her and took the cap off the Sharpie beside her. "How do you spell your name?"

Kelsi spelled it, and then she walked closer. "I've loved your show since the first episode. I'm totally addicted, and I have most of them memorized."

Shane nodded. "She's not kidding. I was required to watch the show with her while we were dating."

"It's great to meet such a big fan," Valerie said, handing her the photograph. "Make sure to come and do a picture with us during the last hour of the party."

"Oh, I will!" Kelsi said. She walked down the line, talking to all the stars, her face so happy. When she finished, she spotted Michelle and hurried over. "I can't believe they're really here!"

Michelle laughed. "Well, you did make it a stipulation of the ranch being used for Steven's next project. I don't think anyone felt like they had a choice."

Kelsi shrugged. "I brought more income to the ranch and made people in the whole area happy with that idea. It was brilliant, wasn't it?"

"Sure was. I'm glad you did it, Kelsi." Michelle was thrilled that Kelsi was so unbelievably happy to meet people she'd idolized for years. It was fun to watch her. "Have you met Bob Bodefeld's wife, May?"

Kelsi nodded. "I actually met her before she was Bob's wife. Jolene Gold, right?"

May nodded. "I met Bob about a week after I left the ranch." She leaned forward and whispered, "And I did my best not to fangirl all over him. I'm one of the founding members of Team Bob."

"I had no idea! Why didn't we talk *Lazy Love* for hours upon hours while you were here before?" Kelsi asked.

"Because I was here for a writing retreat with Kaya and Liz. Kaya met Glen that week, but all of us were writing as fast as we could to finish up books."

"Ahh...well, that makes sense. I'm going to go see what looks yummy."

Shane nodded to Michelle and May as he was pulled away by his exuberant little wife.

"I guess she's happy," Michelle said with a grin.

"Is she really the reason we're all here?"

"Yes. She is the youngest of the six Weston siblings who own the ranch. When the opportunity arose, she made sure she'd get to meet the people she wanted to meet." Michelle shrugged. "Kelsi's more than a little eccentric, but we all love her."

"She seems like a fun person." May's eyes caught someone across the room. "Excuse me. There's someone I have to hug."

Michelle smiled and nodded, watching as May made her way across the room to Kaya and hugged her tight. Both women walked back to her. "We couldn't leave you to wallflower alone!" May told Michelle.

"Thank you. I appreciate it more than you know."

Kaya smiled. "You look wonderful in your new dress. I can't believe we found something that gorgeous and perfect for you in one evening."

"I'm so glad we did. I feel out of place wearing this. Imagine how I would have felt if I hadn't had something glamorous to wear." Michelle looked over her shoulder when she felt a warm hand on her bare back. "Hi, you."

Steven grinned, handing her a cup of punch. "It's pretty good."

Michelle took it and drank it down greedily. It was amazing how thirsty being nervous made her. "Thank you."

"You're very welcome." He looked around the room. "Are you all right? I'm playing host, but you can come right along with me."

"Do you need me?" she asked. "I'm talking with May and Kaya, but they'll be happy to get rid of me."

"I would like to introduce you to some people I know," he said.

She looked around and realized that it wasn't only locals there. There were other people dressed to the nines whom she'd never seen before. Looking to May and Kaya she said, "I'll see you both later. Thanks for wallflowering with me."

"Happy to do it," Kaya said, hugging her quickly. "Just remember you're a beautiful, confident, intelligent woman, and you'll be just fine."

Michelle nodded at the whispered words. "See you soon, I hope."

For the next thirty minutes, Michelle was introduced to many of Stevens co-conspirators on his project. They were all excited that he'd secured the ranch as a place to film.

She smiled and acted polite for each one, but she was very intimidated by all of them. When he'd finally finished introducing her around, he smiled. "You did great!"

"I didn't let them see me sweat!" Michelle grinned at him, and he found himself lost in her eyes.

"I need to go play host some more. Do you want to stay with me, or go back to your wallflowers?"

"Isn't this part of the night almost over? I have a feeling my wallflowers are going to go back to their husbands, and I'll be all alone. Me against the big bad world!" She laid the back of her wrist across her forehead dramatically.

"You planning on trying out for a part in an upcoming movie? You'd make a great fainting lady."

Michelle made a face at him. "No, but I'm going to stick to your side like someone used superglue on us both."

"Hmmm...I think I like that idea. Sounds great to me!"

He walked over toward the stars to let them up from signing autographs. They were sitting quietly anyway, because everyone had finished. "You guys ready to mingle and look happy to be here?"

Valerie shrugged. "I *am* happy to be here. It's a nice place."

The next hour whizzed by for Michelle, because she enjoyed talking to the stars when there were no other people crowded around them. Kelsi became her best friend and stood beside her. She didn't have a lot to say to the stars, but she soaked up every word they spoke.

As people took their pictures with the stars, they gradually left the building, and in the end, it was only the stars, May, Steven, Michelle, Kaya, and Kelsi left, along with the staff. Steven let out a breath as the last person who wasn't part of the core group left the building.

"I think that went really well," Steven said. "It was good to get the other people involved with producing the show here. They've been auditioning people in California. We'll be ready to start shooting February first."

Kelsi clapped her hands together. "Another show for me to love!"

"You have to love the one about your family," Kaya said with a grin.

"That's true. I'm just excited that I'll be able to watch it from the beginning...and recognize everything. It's going to be fun."

May smiled. "It will be fun. But I have a little Bobbi who is hanging out at the Kids' Korral who needs her sleep. And I need to feed her before I explode."

Kelsi nodded. "I have twins there right now, and I should feed them soon, too."

"How old are your twins?" May asked.

"Ten months...ten and a half, to be technical. I'm a twin, and it freaked me out a bit when I found out I was having twins, but my twins are fraternal. Dani and I are identical."

Shane waved at Kelsi from across the room. "My sheriff husband is being all forceful about me leaving. I guess I should listen to him for a change..."

Kaya and Michelle laughed as Kelsi wandered off toward Shane. "I need to get home, too. Glen stayed at the ranch to do paperwork tonight, so I'm off to spend a little time with him before he sleeps and I need to start writing for the night." She hugged May. "I will see you in the chat room. I miss our lunches."

"I do too! But I don't know how much time either of us would have now. We have demanding husbands…"

"Hey! Who are you calling demanding?" Bob asked, wrapping his arm around her shoulders.

May grinned at him, and Michelle felt her stomach clench. She wanted what they had. All of the stars had obviously found the loves of their lives. Watching them together tonight had been eye-opening. She'd been convinced that no one could work in the film industry and be faithful, but these people truly loved each other.

When Michelle and Steven said goodbye to the others and she drove him back to his cabin, she felt a burning inside her. She wanted what all his friends had. She wanted the kind of love all the people on the ranch had. She loved Steven the way the others loved each other, but could he love her the same way?

She stopped the car in front of his house, turning to him. "I had a lovely time. It wasn't easy for me, but I think I could do this again."

"You do?" Steven was excited. Did that mean she was saying she was ready to fit into his life?

She nodded. "It was hard. I won't deny that, but wearing a dress didn't kill me, and I enjoyed a few of the people I got to meet."

"A few?" He laughed. "You're never going to mince words with me, are you?"

She shrugged, a grin on her lips. "At least you'll always know where you stand with me."

"I will." He traced her lips with his forefinger, smiling at her. "Do you want to come in and watch an episode of our show? I think it would be a lot of fun for you to watch the show now, with them all still fresh in your mind."

Michelle thought about it for a moment and nodded. "You know, that does sound interesting." And it meant she'd have at least another hour with him. Their time together was coming to an end because he left in less than forty-eight hours, and she wanted to take advantage of every minute she could.

"Let's go, then." He was thrilled she wasn't ready to hurry off and stare at walls, which was what May always said she did after an event. May needed to be in a room alone and stare at walls for a few minutes so she could calm herself and be ready to be with other people again.

She settled onto the couch while he got them both glasses of ice water. When he came around to join her, he handed her a glass and sank down close beside her.

"How are you feeling today? I can't believe I haven't asked that. What kind of doctor am I?"

Steven smiled. "I'm mostly better. There's a little lingering pain, but I think I'm just sore. I'll be all right."

"Did it hurt you walking around as much as you had to tonight?"

He shook his head. "No more than anything else hurts. I'm not going to let falling off a mountain get me down."

She laughed. "Please don't fall off a mountain again!"

He reached for the remote, finding the next episode and starting it. She leaned against him, her head on his shoulder. She wished they could stay that way forever instead of him leaving. Why did the people that mattered always have to leave?

Steven wrapped his arm around her, feeling the pressure of their time together ending. He couldn't leave without some kind of understanding between them, but would she be willing to even discuss a long-term relationship?

He had no idea, but before Sunday was over, he had to find out. There was no way he could leave without at least trying.

Chapter Ten

Michelle woke early the following morning, well aware that it was her last day with Steven. They'd agreed to meet at his cabin, because the actors were leaving that afternoon. She wanted to have a chance to say goodbye. He'd said he'd cook breakfast for everyone, and she'd agreed to stop at the store on her way out to the ranch.

When she got to his cabin, Bob, Jesse, and John came out to help her carry her things in. She was wearing jeans and a t-shirt, and she realized that Steven had never seen her dressed so casually. Hopefully he wouldn't be disappointed in her. Today she was just Michelle. Not Dr. Michelle. Not his date for the big party. She was simply herself. Hopefully he'd like her in normal mode.

Bob, Jesse, and John carried in the groceries, and Michelle wandered in after them. "I could have carried a couple of bags myself."

"Why would you when there are gentlemen around?" Jesse asked her, setting his bags onto the counter.

Nicki hurried over to her. "Now can we play Barbies? I talked Mama into letting me bring them over from my cabin."

Michelle grinned. "I would love to!"

"Yay! Mama plays with me sometimes, but she works a lot and doesn't have much time to sit around playing with my dolls."

"I can see that. I work a lot, too, but this morning, I have time to play for a while." Michelle followed Nicki into the living room, looking at her array of Barbies. There were two Kens and eight Barbies, which Michelle felt was probably unfair to the females, but obviously Nicki didn't mind it. "Which one do I get to play with?"

Nicki thought hard and finally handed Michelle one Ken and one Barbie. "I think those two should have a wedding."

"All right." Michelle looked through the clothes all over the floor, and she had to wonder how much extra her parents had paid to bring along all of her Barbie things so she'd have something to play with. "You have a lot of Barbie stuff!"

"I have more at home, but Mama said I couldn't bring anything but the car and clothes. I think they should have their camper to stay here, but I wasn't allowed. Maybe someday you'll visit me in Texas, and you can play with my fun stuff."

Michelle grinned at the offer. "I'd like that a lot."

"Me too!" Nicki proceeded to start shoving the six dolls in her possession into dresses for the wedding, while Michelle had to fight just one Barbie into a wedding dress. She'd forgotten how hard they were to dress.

When it was time for breakfast, Michelle was happy to finally get off the floor. She was very flexible and could sit on the floor longer than most adults, but it still wasn't her preferred place to be.

Steven had made pancakes, scrambled eggs, and bacon, and he'd provided cheese and tortillas for anyone who wanted to make the breakfast into breakfast burritos. The group was big and noisy as they all ate together, but Michelle realized she felt perfectly at home with these people.

After breakfast, they all sat around and talked for a bit, and Michelle enjoyed getting to know them all a bit more informally. When Steven sat beside her on the couch and wrapped his arm around her shoulders, no one even batted an eye. She realized that everyone was accepting them as a couple. No one thought a thing of them being together.

Once everyone else had left to go and pack, Michelle rolled up the sleeves of her long-sleeved t-shirt and walked into the kitchen. "Let's knock out these dishes before they come back."

He shook his head. "You don't have to help. I'll do it."

"You cooked while I played Barbies. It's the least I can do to help you get it all cleaned up." She ran a sink full of water and started washing, and he picked up a towel and dried.

"I'm leaving shortly after lunch tomorrow," he said softly.

"I hate that it's already time for you to go." She was going to be lost without him, but she didn't tell him that. Guilting him into staying wouldn't make either of them happy.

"Me too. I've done what I set out to accomplish here on the ranch, but I never dreamed I'd find you here."

She nodded, not looking at him as a tear drifted down her face. "And I never thought Bridget would bring me a man I'd fall for." The love of her life. She could think the words, even if she couldn't say them aloud.

"Would you mind if I came back to visit you?" he asked, trying to ease into the real conversation he wanted to have.

"Well, I'm sure you're going to be on and off the ranch for the show."

"That's not what I mean. I want to come here specifically to see you. I don't want to just come here to do the work I need to do." He held his breath as he waited for an answer, his heart pounding wildly in his chest. He'd never had a relationship that had meant a lot to him before, but she meant the whole world.

The door opened then as Jesse and Valerie came back with little Jaron. "I can help with the dishes!" Valerie offered. "You cooked, Steven. You shouldn't have to clean up!"

Michelle wasn't sure if she was happy with the interruption or not. There'd been a lot to talk about, and they needed to discuss it, but she wasn't sure how she was going to be able to answer his question. Was it best to prolong the heartbreak? Or should there be a good clean break now to avoid that later?

Valerie happily dried the dishes, talking a bit about how much she loved the ranch. "You need to come out to Wyoming where we live now. Every time we have a break on the show, we fly there. It's a small town, and we just love the community. My sister lives there too."

Steven had filled Michelle in a little on what had happened to her sister. "How's she doing?"

"Really well. She married a pastor a little over a year ago. He's been wonderful for her. They really do belong together."

"I'm so glad. Steven told me what happened to her—and you—and I worried there were lasting scars."

Valerie frowned. "I think she'll always have scars. My part in it was short, and Jesse was there to help me within minutes. She was tied up for a couple of days. It was awful."

"I'm so sorry. What happened to the guy?"

"He's in prison. Serving a life sentence, and we hope it really lasts that long." Valerie wiped a dish and set it on the counter. "I dated him for years. I was afraid to try to get away. And then one day, I just knew it was time and I had to or he'd kill me."

"I'm so sorry."

Valerie glanced over her shoulder to where Jesse was holding Jaron and talking to Steven. "I'm not. It made me strong. I don't think I'd have been ready for my happily ever after with Jesse if I hadn't had that terrible experience with Curtis. All water under the bridge now." She shrugged. "Have you ever heard the saying 'Love can heal all wounds?' It's true in my case. Jesse healed me in a way I didn't believe was possible."

"That's really sweet. You two seem to have amazing chemistry on the show."

Valerie laughed. "Fans were begging us to marry by the end of season one. We made them wait months for the first kiss on the show."

"And they dragged it out?"

Valerie nodded. "They were worried it would hurt the ratings if we married on the show, but when I got pregnant, they decided to write marriage and baby into the script. So much easier than me having to hold things in front of my belly and all the other tricks to hide the pregnancy."

"Makes sense." Michelle handed her another glass to dry. "I'm really glad I got to meet you. You're not nearly as scary as I thought a television star would be."

"I try not to be scary. I don't even hide from my fans."

"I think that's neat."

The front door opened again, and May and Bob came in. "Do you need help?" May asked, handing Bobbi to Bob.

"Nah, we're almost done," Michelle answered.

"Then I'm going to stick in here and talk to you two. Bobbi is fussy, and every time I get within three feet of her she wants to nurse, even though she's not hungry. It's Bob's turn to mess with her."

"Is he going to whip one out and feed her?" Valerie asked, her eyes dancing.

"I sure hope not. We do not need naked Bob this morning."

After the dishes were finished, Amber walked in with John and Nicki. They all met up in the living room. "I can't believe you guys are already leaving," Michelle said. "I was just getting to know you!"

Amber frowned at her. "You'll have to come visit the set in Texas. We all want to see you again. Our house is big enough...you could even stay with us."

"I'm not sure that's going to happen, but I really do appreciate the offer."

Steven frowned at that, but said nothing. Their talk would have to happen after the others had left. "All right. Let's all get to the landing strip so you guys can head back to Texas."

"You're directing next week, right?" Valerie asked. "You're my favorite director, but don't tell the others!"

"I won't!" Steven grinned. Valerie told him that constantly, but he had a feeling she told the other directors the same thing.

An hour later, the others had been seen off, and they were back in his cabin. "Now, back to what we were discussing before."

Michelle looked down at the floor, her eyes filling with tears. "I don't want to talk about you leaving yet."

"We need to." He reached out and took her hand, pulling her over to the couch. "I don't want to leave you here. Come with me."

"What? I can't just leave everything. My practice..."

He frowned at that. "With as much as I travel, I don't know if there would be a way for you to have a practice. I know you went to school for a long time. Could you possibly work when we're here?"

"We? Steven, I can't just make a decision that quickly..." She wanted to take off and travel with him, but it would destroy her mother if she lived with a man she wasn't married to.

"I can't imagine spending my life without you. I can make this my home base and come back when I'm between projects." He took a deep breath. "I love you, Michelle. Please marry me? That's the first step here, I think, because..."

She blinked at him a few times, tuning out everything he was saying after he asked her to marry him. She flew at him, wrapping her arms around him and holding him close. "I love you, too!"

"And the other part of what I said? The 'Will you marry me?' part? Do you have an answer to that?"

She nodded. "I'll marry you. We'll work out the details later. I can travel with you if we're married."

He held her to him. "Really? You'll marry me? What's the waiting period in Idaho?"

"There isn't one..."

"No waiting period? I'll marry you tomorrow. Can you come with me when I go back to California? I promise I'll let you live here, but I need a little bit of a honeymoon."

She smiled, nodding. "I have a friend who can fill in for me. He really wants my job, so maybe I can just let him take over."

"You mean it?"

"I do. It wasn't traveling and not working that was bothering me. It was the idea of traveling with you without being married to you."

"I would never ask that of you!" Steven shook his head at her. "You'll really marry me?"

"I really will."

He sighed, holding her against him. "I sure hope Pastor Kevin doesn't have any plans tomorrow..."

"I know something about Pastor Kevin that you don't. He secretly cheers for every single couple that marries on this ranch. He's going to be willing to do it, with no problem."

"Good. Because I'd marry you today if I could get a license."

She frowned. "Does this mean I have to go shop for another formal dress?"

"Borrow Kaya's."

Michelle grinned. "You know what? I think I will!"

Steven smiled. "I have a tux ready and waiting."

"Then I'll call now, and we'll set it up for tomorrow. Let's not invite a thousand of our most intimate friends, though, okay?"

"How 'bout we have you, me, Bridget and Kaya? That would work for me."

"We'd better invite Jaclyn and Kelsi..."

He laughed, feeling as if he was a new man. "Absolutely. Anyone you want." As long as she was willing to be his wife, he'd be willing to do just about anything. Who would have thought falling off a mountain could make a man so happy?